MW01320941

Forgotten Treasures

25 Short Fiction Stories

By Lisa Kessler

Hope you enjoy the stories Cassandra!

Lisa Kessler

This book is a work of fiction. Names, characters, places, and incidents are the product of the author's imagination or are used fictitiously. Any resemblance to actual events, locales, or persons, living or dead,
is coincidental.

Copyright © 2011 by Lisa Kessler. All rights reserved, including the right to reproduce, distribute, or transmit in any form or by any means.

Cover design by: ParaGraphic Designs
Cover Art by: Panda Wilson
Edited by: Jennifer Morris
ISBN 13: 978-0615567228

Manufactured in the United States of America

*This book is dedicated to Ray Bradbury.
Without his challenge to write
52 stories in 52 weeks,
Many of these tales may never have come to light.*

Author's Note

Short stories were my first love in school. I remember reading The Lottery and The Most Dangerous Game for the first time, and being shocked at the emotions they inspired. Later I moved on to Edgar Allen Poe, Ray Bradbury and Stephen King and marveled at the ability they had to make characters come alive in so few words.

I was lucky enough to meet Ray Bradbury a few years ago, and I was struck by his passion for his craft. He actually made me cry when he talked about how deeply he loved writing.

Love. Fall in love and stay in love. Write only what you love, and love what you write. The key word is love. You have to get up in the morning and write something you love, something to live for. – Ray Bradbury

He gave me some amazing advice. He challenged me to write 52 short stories in 52 weeks. At first, I ignored his advice. I'd sold short stories before, and there wasn't much money in it.

Then I realized that money couldn't be the motivator. It was love. Pure love.

And every week I wrote.

As the year went by and I looked over the mass of stories, I realized what a gift he'd given me. Story after story, filled with new characters and places. His challenge helped make magic for me as a writer.

More importantly, he reminded me why I write.

The answer is simple…

Love.

Table of Contents:

Afraid of the Dark

The Curse of Hamelin	1
Invaded	11
Outbreak	19
Hunted	28

Forgotten Treasures

The Diva	38
My Prison	45
The Chariot Race	49

Demons and More

A Demon on the Drums	62
Internet Dating Secrets	69
The Bet	74

Sci-Fi Tales

Going Home	83
Desert Storm	90
Invaders	102

Fantasy

The Aviator	108
In the Dead of Winter	115
Unemployed Muses Anonymous	121

Love and Loss

Last Dance	131
Stranded	138
The Mission	150

Halloween

A Pirate's Treasure	164
1530 Archibald Street	181
The Caretaker	189

Christmas

The Third King	199
The Business Trip	212
The Demon's Christmas	222

The Curse of Hamelin

They were coming.

He couldn't see them yet; he sensed them. The scent of moist tilled earth teased his nostrils, and bile rose in response.

How did this happen again so soon?

Harold made a frantic dash to the dresser and yanked open the drawers. He needed to get out fast. Snatching up his pressed and folded clothes, he placed them on the tidy bedspread and reached under the ruffled bed skirt for his suitcase.

Something grabbed his hand.

Harold squealed, and tugged, trying to free his limb. "No please! Let me go!"

Wet, guttural cackling answered him from

under the bed.

His heart slammed in his chest, and a slick sheen of perspiration spread across his face. "Who– Who's there? Please, just let me go."

A heavy bead of sweat ran down his forehead, along the curve of his nose, and finally dripped onto the front of his white dress shirt, distracting him from the impending doom lurking under the bed. With his free hand, Harold fumbled at the sweat stain, frantic to get the spot out.

The thing under the bad gripped his wrist tighter and yanked, slamming Harold's head against the mattress. Snapped out of his compulsive sweat-stain cleaning, he tugged back.

"Let- me- go!" Harold wrenched his hand free, stumbling backwards into the desk chair of his hotel suite.

The thing under the bed hissed, filling the air with a stale putrid stench, and Harold gagged. Forget the clothes. He'd buy more. Racing for the dresser, he grabbed his keys and cell phone and spun toward the door.

"Oh my God!" He gasped.

The thing from under the bed now blocked his only exit. Wisps of fine white hair poked out from beneath the black hooded robe, and gnarled gray hands protruded from the oversized sleeves. One of the bony digits rose up to point at him.

"You cannot escape your destiny, Harold

Frommer."

The sound of its voice raised the hair on his arms. "How do you know my name?"

"I know who you really are. Why are you still living a lie? You are the chosen one. They rise for you."

Harold shook his head. "Don't say that! I never asked for this curse."

The thing from under the bed tossed his head back and let out a vile hacking laugh. The hood slid back, revealing his weather-beaten, rotting face. Its pallid, translucent skin exposed clogged veins and arteries which no longer transported blood. Harold took a step backward; wincing when the thing's thin lips drew back to reveal chipped remains of what might have at one time been teeth.

"A curse?" It took a step toward him. "You are descended from a proud line of Pipers. This is your gift. We cannot resist your song. Why do you run from us?"

"I– I don't sing," he stammered. "Just go away. How do you keep finding me?"

"I already told you, we cannot resist. You call to us from beyond the grave."

"No, no I don't. Just leave me alone."

"We will always find you." The thing glared at him. "You can't run from your destiny by moving from one place to another."

"Is that from Hemingway?" Harold nodded. "I think it is Hemingway. I never figured out why I needed to read Hemingway for a degree in accounting, but literature was an undergraduate requirement."

The thing tilted its head, and for a moment, Harold thought its skull might break free from the pencil neck that held it upright. Either way, it distracted him from his obsessive ramblings long enough for him to notice the growing stains expanding from his armpits.

His hands trembled.

He couldn't wear a filthy, dirty shirt. But he didn't have time to change.

"What are you doing, Piper?"

"Stop calling me that." Harold fiddled to free each button. He wriggled out of his shirt and let out a sigh of relief. "I can't wear a stained shirt."

In the distance, he heard the muffled screams of hotel guests. They were closer now. The thing from under the bed turned toward the sound, and Harold quickly reached down to grab his suitcase. When he straightened, the thing was right in front him. Harold gasped and held the bag up between them.

"Leave me alone."

"I cannot leave you, Piper. None of us can."

"That's not my fault." He backed up a step.

"No, it is your gift." It rubbed its gnarled hands together. "Your heritage."

Harold looked over his shoulder. From his third story window, he could see them coming. Deformed, decaying bodies lurched forward toward the hotel. It was happening again.

When he turned eighteen the dead started following him. It wasn't so bad at first. While he attended college he only had one dead stalker following him. But each year, the silent "song" they claimed to hear grew stronger. He couldn't stay in one city for more than two days before the dead ripped their decayed bodies free from their graves and came to find him.

The smell alone was bad, but actually seeing their filthy rotting bodies sent his OCD into overdrive. No amount of medication could convince him his hands or his clothes were clean enough after encountering one of the dead.

Now nearly a hundred skeletal bodies with dirt clots falling free from the remaining tufts of dried hair gathered in the street. Skin hanging limply like peeling wallpaper, exposing the bones underneath. They stumbled and lurched toward his hotel. Harold's hand started to tremble and his lower eyelid twitched.

He turned away from the window when he heard more screams. The dead were inside the building now. His gaze flicked to the thing from under the bed.

"Zombies are not my heritage."

His watery gray filmed eyes glittered. "Each generation of Piper sings its own song. You call to lost souls. Dead souls."

"Necromancers don't exist," Harold screamed.

It pointed a bony finger toward the window. "They have returned to their bodies and follow your song, Piper."

Harold gazed out the window again. Dead bodies filled the parking lot. Cars honked, some actually plowed through the throngs of the dead, sending skeletal bodies bouncing across the pavement.

This was his fault.

Years ago, when the dead first started surfacing, Harold researched his ancestry. His family originated from Germany, but he was surprised when he found that they actually came from a small village called, Hamelin.

The oldest story from the town was the Tale of the Pied Piper of Hamelin who played a melody that the rats couldn't resist. He led them to the river where they drowned. When the town refused to pay for his services, he led the children away.

They were never found.

Since then, every other generation of his

family was a "Piper" of some sort. His grandfather was forced to live in a cabin in Montana because wolves were constantly drawn to him. His great-grandfather before him could call hawk. The list went on and on, but nowhere in his family tree had the Hamelin curse called the dead.

Not until Harold.

After researching necromancers, the horror of his curse became clear. Since then he traveled from place to place, living out of his suitcase, trading stocks online to earn a living until it was time to move on.

How much longer could he run?

He stared at the hideous thing again, and shoved it back with his suitcase. "I need to go."

"You know what will happen if you leave."

"I can't stay here."

"They will die."

"They're already dead!" Harold screamed, wringing his hands. He needed to scrub. Hot water, boiling hot water and soap, lots of soap, he could almost smell the soap. Almost. But the scent of soil and decay overpowered it.

With a burst of adrenaline, he chucked his suitcase at the withered thing from under the bed and raced for the door. He yanked it open, wincing at the sound of the tongueless wails echoing through the hallway. They were already on the third floor!

Harold ran the other way, away from the main elevators. He threw open the door and peered down the stairwell. It looked clear. He jogged down the stairs without touching the germ-infested, dirty handrail. Just because something looked clean didn't mean it was.

When he reached the bottom, he barely pulled the door open to peek outside. Most of the bodies were heading for the main entrance. If he hurried, he could get to his rental car before they realized he was outside.

He took a deep breath and burst through the door, scrambling to his rental car. The cold air hit him hard, like the shock of jumping into a cold swimming pool, but he kept running. He wished he had his shirt and jacket, but he would buy another one in the next city. For now he just had to get away.

The locks popped up as he neared the car, and Harold hopped inside. One of the dead turned his way and let out a lipless cry to the others. A group of corpses turned, lumbering toward him. Harold fired up the engine, slammed the car into reverse and gunned the accelerator. Two of the walking dead bounced off his bumper as he switched into drive and raced forward.

He was free.

He wiped the nervous sweat from his forehead and glanced into the rearview mirror. The corpses were already falling, one by one. They flopped onto the ground into decaying heaps, lifeless once more. Harold stared straight ahead and gripped the steering wheel. He wondered how this town would explain that half of the cemetery got up and walked into the Marriott today.

It was always interesting to see scientists and local law enforcement try to explain the unexplainable.

But what could they say?

Even Harold didn't know how necromancy worked. He didn't *try* to bring the dead souls back to their rotting corpses. He didn't know why they flocked to him, or why they lost control of their corpses when he left the area.

He only knew it was getting more and more impossible to live a normal life. Maybe that was why the dead followed him. Maybe they would see to it that he never married and fathered children.

Maybe the Curse of Hamelin was meant to die with him.

And then, everything was clear. Everything.

He didn't need a clean shirt, and for the first time in his life, his hands felt clean. Harold pressed down on the accelerator until his foot hit the floor, and once the speedometer passed the sixty mile-per-hour mark, he angled the wheel on a collision course with a telephone pole.

Less and than ten seconds later, the Curse of Hamelin was no more.

Neither was Harold Frommer.

The End

Invaded

It started with the new hip.

Becky teetered on the edge of the bridge. Sweat dripped down her face while she danced through the pain in her hip. This would be her final performance. She would accept nothing less than perfection.

Her worn ballet shoes scraped against the concrete as a gust of cool night air caressed her skin through her black leotard and snagging purple leg-warmers. The cadaver bone transplant in her new hip was poisoning her. She knew that now. Blood stained her hands to prove it.

"Don't think about it!" She growled to herself as she spotted her pirouettes.

Instead, she thought about her high school graduation. It seemed like a lifetime ago. She didn't excel in school, but she got by. High school stood as the final hurdle before dream of dancing with a professional ballet company could come true.

That last hurdle.

On graduation day, with her diploma in hand, she ran toward the stands to greet her family, but the heel of her shoe caught in the hem of her gown. Her square cap went flying as she crashed down onto the concrete steps of the bleachers. Pain shot up her right leg like a bullet, shooting stars around the edge of her vision.

That was the day Becky Tildon's life changed forever.

After staring at x-rays of Becky's cracked and splintered hip, and meeting with two top orthopedic specialists, the doctors presented Chuck Tildon with two options.

They recommended repairing the hip joint with a titanium replacement, but they also cautioned that because of his daughter's young age, the metal joint would need to be replaced, possibly every fifteen years.

It was likely she would face many surgeries through her life.

"What's the other option?" he asked.

The doctors looked at one another before

Dr. Garrison replied, "It's a bit more costly and it may delay the surgery to repair the hip."

Becky looked at the three men in her room. The silence seemed to last an eternity.

"So what is it?" Becky asked.

"A cadaver bone transplant to repair the hip." Dr. Garrison glanced from her to her father.

Chuck Tildon's brow furrowed. "Cadaver? As in a dead body? You want to put a bone from a dead body inside my daughter?"

"It's actually a very good option considering Becky's age. Often over time the patient's own bones will grow and fuse around the transplant, and the body rarely rejects the new bone. This way she could avoid future surgeries to replace the joint."

Becky pressed the button to lift up the back of her bed. "Could I dance again?"

"Only time will tell," Dr. Garrison answered. "It's certainly a possibility."

Becky heard all she needed. She talked her father into the cadaver bone transplant, and within two months she was back in the dance studio, gradually rehabilitating her hip.

Her muscles were slow to recover, and before long her patience wore thin. Her hip was often stiff, forcing her to walk with a limp, and finding a comfortable position to sleep challenged her every night.

Vicodin became her best friend.

She loathed her addiction, and at the same time craved the numbness it promised. It made no sense. She'd always prided herself on her self-discipline and steadfast workout schedule for dance. Why couldn't she focus anymore?

She struggled with her inner battle, fighting to keep the pill bottle at bay, but her hands twitched, and her bones ached for relief. Sleeping seemed to be her only refuge until the dreams began. Dreams of a tall, broad-shouldered man on a bridge. Frequently he threw something off the bridge into the river below. Something large.

"No more dreams," she promised herself. "Just keep dancing."

She shifted her feet into fifth position and bent her knees into a plié. A bead of sweat rolled down her back as police cars pulled up at either end of the bridge. When they called for her to move back, away from the edge of the bridge, she lifted her right leg up behind her into an arabesque. This used to be one of her best moves, but now the pain was so sharp she almost whimpered, her leg trembled with effort.

Their floodlights splashed white light over her. She lifted her body, balancing on the tip of her toe shoe. Swan Lake played in her head, the floodlights from the patrol cars became spotlights, the bridge her stage, and the uniformed officers her audience.

Her final curtain. The perfect performance for a murderess.

Her leg came down as her arm raised up in a graceful arc. Blood still stained the inside of her wrist. No matter how much she scrubbed it wouldn't fade. It was ironic considering the sight of blood used to make her sick.

That was before the Vicodin and the cadaver bone.

Last week she noticed she couldn't account for a few hours in the afternoon. At first she hadn't been concerned. All her days seemed fuzzy now that she lived in a pain-killer haze. She'd probably been napping. But as the week progressed, she was missing more than just time.

"Don't go there," she whispered, as a tear spilled down her cheek.

Her jaw tightened, fighting to hold back the emotions. Her legs tensed, tired muscles pulled her up into relevé making her toes cramp against the thin pad inside the tip of her toe shoes. The police called to her again, coaxing her with false promises of forgiveness and understanding. Instead of running to them, her toes danced along the edge of the bridge with tiny steps. Her bourrees were the envy of all the other girls in the dance studio.

The dance studio.

Her Dad came in that afternoon to talk to

her about some of the younger girls she mentored. Apparently two were missing. Had she seen them? Of course not.

But someone else said she had. They said they saw her with the girls riding in the backseat of her car, driving them toward the city. Over the bridge. This bridge.

"No!" Her chest heaved with a sob. She lowered into a plié.

It was only a dream. She'd seen the man in her dreams. He took children to the bridge. He didn't mean to hurt them. But he did. He killed them and tossed their lifeless bodies off the bridge into the swift current of the river below.

And he lived inside her now.

She could feel him polluting her bloodstream, weak, begging for the release that the drugs promised, and for the love young flesh offered. With his hip implanted in her body, his desires festered and spread like a virus.

When the dreams first began haunting her, she'd been curious. She suddenly craved beer, although she'd never liked the taste before, let alone the calories. It made no sense. So she searched for answers. What she found terrified her.

Cellular memory. Case after case of transplant patients who experienced this strange phenomenon. For some it was simple. They now enjoyed a food that they'd never tolerated before the transplant. In other cases the patient was suddenly drawn to classical music only to find that their donor had been a concert violinist.

But what if your donor murdered small children?

Her cadaver bone came from a middle-aged man killed in a car accident. That was the only information the hospital shared with her. But now she knew far more about him than the doctors. His toxic urges invaded her body, mixing with and mutating her own.

Her stomach wretched as she remembered the two blond sisters in their pink tutus. Their hair smelled like baby shampoo. They were filled with infectious giggles and toothless grins. And now a bloody rag littered her trunk.

What had she done? She scrubbed the evidence from under her fingernails, but she couldn't dig his poison out of her bones.

There was only one solution.

She stepped off the edge of the bridge toward the police, but spun back as they approached her. With two graceful running strides, she launched herself into the air, executing a graceful Grand jeté, floating over the edge of the bridge.

She hadn't achieved such a perfect split jump since the accident at her high school graduation.

    Becky smiled as she fell into oblivion.
    Dance was her life... And her death.

The End

Outbreak

Her barefooted common-law husband raised the cast iron skillet over his head, stalking his prey. From the porch of the rusted trailer, she waited. What was taking him so long?

"It's gonna slither away, Earl. Whack it already!"

"Shut up woman…" He barked over his shoulder, still eyeing his quarry. "This don't look like no gopher snake. Damn thing is bright yellow."

"The color don't matter none, Earl. Just kill it."

The cast iron skillet hit the earth with a

resounding crunch. Earl screamed, "I got it!"

She grinned exposing a missing tooth in her smile. "Bring it up here. I got the pot all ready."

Earl carried the lifeless snake in one hand and the bloodied skillet in the other. He handed his wife the limp reptile. "You owe me big time for this one, Daisy. She's a beaut."

Daisy nodded with a smile. "You done good, Earl."

***

Dr. Dan Greenbauer feverishly pounded at his computer keyboard. A bead of sweat rolled down his forehead as he checked over his shoulder. He had to be careful. His experiments were top secret. If they caught him erasing some of the data, he wasn't sure what they'd do. His life wasn't nearly as important as his work. No one would ever find his body if he died here.

He shuddered and turned back to his computer screen.

He'd been working a mile underground at the Dulce Base in New Mexico for six months now. Virus mutations were his specialty. Down in his lab on level six, he recorded data on his experiments with the animals.

Simple. Or at least it used to be.

Until he lost a seven foot long Coastal Taipan snake.

One of the world's most venomous snakes

had been missing for two days. At first, he was sure Pam, as he called her, slithered into a warm spot in a corner somewhere, but after searching all of level six, he still couldn't find her.

She was a huge yellow snake. She should've been easy to spot, and yet he'd found no trace of the reptile. As the days passed, he was convinced someone stole her. How else could she have escaped from a bunker a mile underground?

But who would have taken her? Without any proof, he couldn't accuse anyone else, and it would only be a matter of time until he was the chief suspect.

So today he was racing to erase all data that referred to the snake. They'd never know he experimented on a Coastal Taipan. He hoped.

He'd been injecting venomous snakes with mutated strains of the Hepatitis C virus to alter the snake's venom. Carrying a lethal version of Hepatitis C, the Coastal Taipan snake could bite and inject her improved venom numerous times. No amount of anti-venom would save a victim of her bite. The mutated strain of Hepatitis C was so potent that it caused acute liver failure within hours instead of days, making the snake a perfect vessel for the government to execute an untraceable assassination.

And now the snake was gone.

Dr. Greenbauer erased the final file. There

were no longer any records of the venomous snake experiments. No record Pam had ever been in the animal lab. He prayed the snake was dead.

She was far too dangerous to be unleashed into the world.

Through his ongoing research, the Hepatitis C strain that Pam carried wasn't just blood-borne anymore. Dr. Greenbauer had chemically engineered the virus to be orally transferred too. Touching her skin and forgetting to wash your hands before you ate your sandwich could kill you.

She was by far the most deadly snake on earth.

And for anyone who was infected, there would be no cure.

***

"Stew smells good, Daisy," Earl walked out the screen door and onto the porch to greet Ed and Loralee. "So where's the kids?"

"Ely broke his toe again, so Georgia's stayin' home with him." Ed lifted his sweat-stained ball cap, scratching his head before tugging it back into place. "We promised to bring back some viddles for 'em."

Earl nodded, hooking his thumb toward the house. "Daisy's makin' a fine snake stew."

"She need any help?" Loralee peeked through the rusted screen.

"Nah," Earl said. "She's got it."

A dented old Ford pick-up backfired, and five teens jumped out of the bed of the truck. Larry Sims turned off the engine. The truck knocked and pinged as he got out. "Baby's not ready to stop drivin' yet!" He laughed.

Earl grinned. "Fords don't run on moonshine, Larry. It's gonna be sputterin' all night."

Larry stared at his truck, just as the final ping sounded. He looked up at Earl and chuckled. "Nah, she's good now. What smells so good?"

"Snake stew," Daisy announced as she lugged a big steam pot out onto the porch. She smacked Earl's hand off the ladle. "Not yet, we got more folks comin'."

***

Jade hated this part of her nursing job. She enjoyed saving lives in the ER, but seeing the aftermath, when they failed, was tough to handle. Doctors delivered the bad news and walked away. Nurses witnessed the pain firsthand.

"I'm so sorry, Mrs. Holt."

She grasped her husband's cool hand, unwilling to let him go. "I can't believe he's gone. He's been bitten before, but..." She wiped a tear and took a shaky breath. "Why didn't the anti-venom work?"

Jade slid his chart back into the plastic

sleeve at the end of the bed. "We're not sure. He tested positive for Hepatitis C, so maybe the anti-venom caused a drug interaction of some kind. We'll know more after the autopsy."

Mrs. Holt frowned. "Gary didn't have Hepatitis."

"He probably didn't show any outward symptoms."

"No, he had a blood work up for his physical last month. He handles a lot of exotic animals with PETA, so his doctor keeps a close watch on him," she said. "He didn't have Hepatitis. They gave him a clean bill of health."

A man poked his head in the door. "Excuse me, Jade?"

She looked up at the orderly. "I'm busy here."

"I know, but the guy who brought in Mr. Holt is back. They need you in Trauma 2."

"Something's wrong with Henry?" Mrs. Holt asked.

"Please excuse me." Jade hustled from the room.

She yanked on a new pair of latex gloves at the door of Trauma 2, and shoved her way through the door.

"He's in hyper-acute liver failure." The doctor said, calling out orders for IVs and medications. "We're losing him."

Jade's brow furrowed. "He was fine when he came in earlier. No sign of jaundice."

"I'm aware of that, Jade," the doctor replied. "Need to tell me anything else I don't already know?"

She ground her teeth together and let the insult slide. "Did he get bitten too?"

"No sign of snakebite. I'm not sure what's going on here..."

Jade stepped back. Her vision narrowed, head spinning. Did she have a fever? She turned to leave the room, but before she reached the door the room went black.

***

Daisy ladled up generous helpings of the snake stew to the sizeable group of friends and relatives from the local church, taking pride in all the compliments on her cooking.

"Earl here, kilt the snake for me," she said.

"Nah, don't be givin' me none of the credit, Daisy. You were the one who turned the yellow thing into a feast."

"You found a yellow snake?" Gil Smith asked.

"Yeah. Never seen one like 'er before. Daisy spotted 'er slitherin' across the drive." He held his arms outstretched to demonstrate his point. "Damn thing was at least six or seven feet long."

Daisy set down the pot and wiped her brow. "I'm not feelin' so good. I better go lay down."

Earl frowned. "But you never miss stew night."

"I know. I'll have some later, doncha worry 'bout me."

"All right."

Daisy retreated back into the trailer. By the time she reached the bedroom, her vision clouded. She fell onto the bed and closed her eyes, not realizing they'd never open again.

***

Dr. Greenbauer tossed back another shot of whiskey as he watched the television news reports. It was happening. The Jicarilla Emergency Center was quarantined with a deadly Hepatitis C outbreak, and there was another report of twenty more dead in a nearby trailer park community. Apparently one of the dead at the ER had been bitten by a snake. No one knew how the rest of the dead contracted the disease.

But Dr. Greenbauer did.

He'd also erased all the data files while hiding evidence of the missing snake. The only files which might have held a cure for the fast-acting virus.

This was his fault.

One lost snake led to a massive outbreak.

He prayed it would stay contained in Dulce, New Mexico. What if someone got on an airplane?

A sob escaped him, guilt strangling any glimmer of hope. He couldn't help them. While covering his own ass, he'd doomed innocent people to death. He never dreamed any of this would happen.

All because of a lost snake.

Tossing back one last shot of whiskey; he raised his revolver and slid the barrel between his teeth. A tear rolled down his cheek.

One snake. One bullet.

He pulled the trigger.

The End

Hunted

They never should have drilled the new well. Something lived down there. Something pure evil. And it was getting closer.

Connie clenched the hands of her two small pajama-clad children, tugging them down the hill, praying they wouldn't make a sound. She winced in the darkness each time her bare feet came down on something sharp.

There wasn't time to grab shoes when they left the house.

They needed to hurry. Her head start wouldn't last long. He was already searching for them, and he wasn't slowed by a five year old son and four year old daughter.

Tears filled her eyes, but there wasn't time for crying. They had to keep moving. Behind them, a furious scream ripped through the silence of the night. He must've found their empty beds. Time was running out.

She scooped Cara up onto her hip in an effort to hurry their pace. Her little girl rubbed her eyes, and for a moment, Connie almost convinced herself this was just a nightmare. She would wake up and find Cara toddling into the kitchen for breakfast and Saturday morning cartoons.

"Ow! Mommy, my foot..."

The sound of her son's voice reminded her that this was no dream. They were living this nightmare.

Ignoring the ache in her back and the screaming pain in her bleeding bare feet, Connie picked up her son, placing him on her other hip as she stumbled through the darkness.

"We can't stop now, honey," she whispered frantically. "We have to keep going."

Matthew looked back over her shoulder while she fought to keep her balance, pushing herself down the hill toward the street.

"He's coming after us, isn't he?" Her little boy asked.

"Yes, baby, but we'll be fine. Don't look back."

But oh how she longed to check behind them. She wanted to know how close he was. She wanted to keep her children safe. Alive.

"I'm scared," Matthew whispered.

"Don't be scared. I'll keep you safe."

"That's Daddy's job." Cara mumbled against her other shoulder.

Blinking back tears, Connie nodded. "I know, but Daddy's not here right now."

Not yet anyway, she thought to herself.

Straight ahead she saw the street. The Henry's ranch was about two-hundred yards away. They'd be safe there, and she'd call the police.

His heavy strides broke through the brush behind her. She heard him coming. Connie stumbled forward, forcing herself to run. She clutched her children close to her body, fighting the fatigue in her legs. He was too fast. They'd never make it. Ducking into the thick underbrush, she lowered Matthew and Cara to the ground.

"Matt, take your sister and run to the Henry's place. Run and never look back."

He nodded and took his sister's hand. For a moment, he looked exactly like his father.

Before the thing in the well stole his soul.

Her eyes shone with tears when she kissed each soft cheek goodbye. "I love you... Now run to the Henry's place. Don't look back, just run, okay?"

Matthew looked much older than any five year old should ever have to. He clutched his sister's pudgy hand in his, and Connie watched them disappear.

With a deep breath, she spun around, and ran back toward her house, toward the monster who used to be the man she loved.

He wasn't their protector anymore. He was the hunter, and they were his prey. She needed to draw him away from their children to buy them a little more time to get to safety.

His hand clutched the back of her hair, and he yanked her in close.

"Where are they?" He spat with labored breath.

"Safe..."

"Bitch!" He threw her to the ground and plowed forward toward the street with his shotgun in hand.

"No!" Connie screamed, stumbling after him. Her heart pounded in her ears, but her fear vanished. Her instinct to protect her children took over.

They were all that mattered.

She ran and dove forward, driving her shoulder into his back, connecting with his kidney. His towering form crumpled to the ground, taking Connie with him.

He rolled over, pinning her beneath him.

She stared up into his face. Hatred, rage, and madness burned in his eyes. His features that used to look at her with love now twisted, contorting into a cold glare.

This wasn't her husband. Not anymore.

"You can't stop me," he growled, and punctuated his statement with his fist.

Never in her life had she been punched in the face. Blood filled her mouth and blackness crept around the edges of her field of vision. He grunted as he rose to his feet, and his boot connected with her ribs, knocking all the air from her lungs. Connie struggled to stay alert. She rolled onto her side, coughing out blood that choked her.

He snatched up his gun and walked toward the street, toward their children.

Her fingernails dug into the earth as she forced air back into her body and lurched forward, wincing in pain. She had to stop him. But how?

She scrambled upright and stumbled after him. The ache in her feet was numbed by the fresh pain in her ribs and her jaw.

The crisp night air puffed past her lips leaving behind a fog, proof she still lived. Each stride came faster than the last until she was running again, closing the distance between herself and the monster chasing after her children.

His shirt was almost within reach. If she

dove, she might catch him and pull him down with her. But what if she missed? She struggled onward, pushing her legs, but her foot caught on something and just when she thought she might stop him, she fell.

Connie hit the ground with such force she cried out in pain. He didn't even look back.

Get up, her mind screamed. *You've got to get up!*

Her children's angelic faces filled her thoughts and cemented her resolve. She checked to see what caught her foot and grimaced as she pushed herself up from the ground. A shovel. It wouldn't compete with his shotgun, but it might buy Matthew and Cara some time.

She hobbled to her feet, grabbing the handle of the shovel. He was ahead of her. She forced her body, drenched in sweat, to run.

A mother's will to protect her young.

How far away were the kids now? If they made it to the Henry's ranch, they'd be safe. The Henry's were a kind older couple. They'd noticed the changes in her husband before she did. They warned her to leave while she could.

If only she had listened.

They would believe Matthew and Cara. And the Henry's would take whatever measures necessary to stop their father.

But they needed to get there first. With a

last burst of adrenaline, she pushed herself faster. She gained on him as she came over the crest of the hill.

Just a few more steps.

She screamed, heaving the shovel, and walloping him in the back of the head. His skull made a sickening hollow thump like a ripe melon, and his body collapsed in a heap onto the ground.

Connie didn't wait. She didn't check. She just ran in the direction of her children. Tears streamed down her face. Did she kill her husband? No, not her husband. Not anymore. He was a monster now.

Without a sound, her progress suddenly halted. He spun her around by her hair and yanked her close to his broken face. Blood trickled from his mouth and nose, one eye bled and the other swelled shut. His bloodied lips curled into a cold sneer. Connie couldn't hold back the scream erupting out of her.

"It'll take more than that to stop me, Bitch."

"Mommeeeeeee!" Her daughter's voice echoed up from the street.

She tried to turn, to see the little one calling her. "Run Baby!"

He punched her stomach so hard she tasted the blood rising in the back of her throat. Instinctively her knee jutted up, embedding into his groin. Again he fell to the ground.

She spun around and yelled, "Run Cara! Don't look back! Just run!"

Silently she prayed they couldn't see her. She wanted them to remember their father for the man he was, not the monster he had become. She didn't want them to see their mother beaten and bloodied.

She searched the darkness. Maybe Cara had only heard her scream. Hopefully Matthew had his little sister nearly to the Henry's ranch by now.

The monster climbed to his feet. Before she ran, his arm jutted out, gripping her by the throat.

"You'll never catch them," she wheezed. "Just take me. Let them go."

"But it doesn't want you." He sneered through bloodied lips. His grip tightened with each word. "It needs the children."

"No!" she squealed, her hand scratching blindly at his face, clawing at his eyes.

He laughed at her efforts and rewarded her with another solid blow to the stomach before dropping her face-first on the ground. He retrieved his shotgun and she closed her eyes.

Instead of shooting her, the butt of the rifle connected with her spine right between her shoulder blades. Pain radiated throughout her entire body.

The metallic taste of blood filled her mouth as she bit the inside of her cheek to keep from crying out. If he thought she was unconscious he might leave her alone, or so she hoped.

He dropped the shotgun, lumbering away from her. Slowly she opened her eyes and reached for the gun.

"Cara, honey! It's Daddy..." he called. "Matthew, come back! Don't be afraid."

Connie's stomach lurched. Bile rose in the back of her throat to hear this monster speak her children's names with her husband's voice. She raised the shotgun up, resting the handle against her aching shoulder. She cocked it, relieved to find shells in the chamber. The sound made him stop and turn around.

"You won't shoot me," he said, walking toward her. "I'm your husband, remember? It's me. We can be happy again, Connie. It only wants the children."

He came closer and her finger tightened on the trigger. The shot sent a death toll through the night and left the roar of silence in its wake.

She dropped the gun beside what remained of his head and stumbled down the hill. Her heart was still racing, and she couldn't keep from glancing back over her shoulder. She needed to get Cara and Matthew. She had to get to them.

She stumbled down the hill toward the

street. Her pulse pounded in her head. A voice encouraged her on; insisted she hurry. Her body ached, but her will was strong.

"Cara! Matthew! It's Mommy... You don't have to run anymore. We're safe now."

She smiled and opened her arms to the small forms racing toward her. It was finally over. Relief filled her with newfound energy. She held them close, breathing in the scent of their hair as she looked back over her shoulder at her house.

A sharp pain shot through her temple. Connie winced and closed her eyes, fighting to clear her head. When she opened them again the pain was receding, and a sudden calm settled over her.

Her purpose was clear.

With a deep breath, she took their tiny hands in hers. "Let's go home."

They walked back quietly, and in the darkness an unfamiliar smile twisted on her face. It still needed her children.

And if her husband couldn't get them for it...

Maybe she could.

THE END

The Diva

    Adella watched from the wings, hidden among the shadows while she awaited her cue.

    Mimi was her signature role, her alter ego for over thirty years. She performed other opera roles during her career, but La Boheme was her bread and butter.

    Night after night, in countries around the world, she brought audiences to their feet with her interpretation of Mimi. Her flawless passion-filled performances of Mi Chiamano Mimi were often collected for Opera anthology recordings, and Sono Andati, the love duet of Rodolfo and Mimi, never failed to make music lovers weep.

But these days it took more effort to achieve what had once erupted from her throat with ease, like a gift from God himself. The last three years she struggled through illnesses, and her smooth legato melody lines were non-existent unless the director allowed her to stand in one place while she sang.

It wasn't for lack of rehearsal. She knew her roles thoroughly, but age was beginning to take its toll. Coloratura roles didn't come her way anymore. She couldn't sustain the fast running cadenzas that used to flow so freely from her lips. She would never sing another Juliet's Waltz from Gounod's Romeo and Juliet.

Would anyone miss her? Ten years ago she reigned in the Opera houses at the pinnacle of her career, the grand Diva of the opera. If she was being considered for a role, other sopranos need not even apply.

But these days, her agent didn't call her to select between competing offers from opera companies. There were new sopranos, rising stars, huddling in the wings, waiting to step into her spotlight.

Enough.

She turned away from the stage and walked back to the prop table. Her mirror with the opal inlay handle sat on the right-hand corner, just where her contract stipulated.

Adella carefully lifted the oval face, checking her lipstick. Stage make-up no longer hid the creases around her eyes, and nothing helped the heaviness below her chin.

She brought her free hand up to her jaw line, smoothing her skin. Recently she noticed opera companies now dressed her in high-necked gowns. Her once thick curls of raven hair spilled down her back, thin and lifeless. The make-up artists added hair extensions and enough hair spray to burn more holes in the ozone layer, just to give her hair the natural look she used to take for granted.

Her grip tightened on the mirror until she felt the handle snap in her hand. Her heart sank and her eyes brimmed with tears. The purchase of the mirror was a splurge to celebrate her first performance at the Metropolitan Opera. Her mirror had been her constant companion throughout her career.

And now it was broken.

She carefully placed the mirror back on the prop table, blinking her eyes to keep the tears at bay. This wasn't the time to get upset. She needed to perform.

For the last time.

Rodolfo finished his aria, and she stepped to her spot in the wings, ready to make the first entrance of her final performance as Mimi from La Boheme. She gently cleared her throat, straightened her dress, and ran her tongue across her top teeth to be certain that no lipstick marred her smile.

The stage manager gave her the silent cue, and Adella stepped out from the shadows. The spotlight felt warm on her skin, and wrapped her in its familiar embrace. Applause exploded from the darkness, and the diva held her head high, expecting and accepting their love and adoration.

When the noise reached its climax, the orchestra overpowered the crowd, silencing them with their melody. Adella and Mimi were once again one spirit, one being, and the music that rose from her throat was more than a song, it was a lifetime.

Music transformed into pure love and joy. Every word was articulated, each note spun forth with the precision of a master, but the effortless sound of an angel.

She enjoyed every second and memorized each moment on the stage. This performance needed to last the rest of her life.

As the fourth and final act opened, Adella found herself in the wings again. She sipped water and handed the glass to one of the stage hands while she watched the other performers on the stage. For months she prepared for this moment.

This would be her final act.

She wasn't ready.

Singing on the stage was her life. There was nothing else. She'd been married once, but her travel schedule soured the union within five years. She had no children, no pets, and all of her friends were still performing.

What would happen to her without dress rehearsals, opening nights, bright lights, the swell of an orchestra, and the swing of the conductor's baton?

There was no turning back. Her voice was showing signs of age. Did she really want to sing until the critics turned against her? Did she want audiences to whisper during intermission about how well she *used to* sing?

No.

She always promised herself she would retire before her voice suffered. She didn't want to become a mockery of what she once was, instead she hoped to be remembered for the standing ovations and operatic beauty of her music.

Now that the end was approaching, her chest ached with sorrow. How could she give up her one true love in this world? This was her life and her identity. Adella Shugart, Soprano. Who would she be when she no longer commanded a stage?

Her cue finally came, and Adella walked

out for the fourth act. How apropos that Mimi's death scene would be her last. For the first time in her career, the tear that rolled down her cheek during the final duet was not an act. Her heart shattered, and the music that escaped her lips echoed her aching soul, as Mimi sang of her love for Rodolfo.

At the end of La Boheme, Mimi knew she was dying. The medicine would not come soon enough to save her. She would leave the world with love in her heart, knowing she was blessed with the love of her Rodolfo.

As the duet reached its final cadence, Mimi collapsed, coughing as consumption stole her breath, and inside Adella sobbed, knowing she delivered the most exquisite performance of her life.

The moment she stepped out to center stage for her final curtain call, the audience rose onto their feet. Chants of "Brava" echoed through the theater as she curtsied and accepted their praises. She waved to the crowd, her cheeks moist with tears she hadn't realized she was shedding. Like Mimi, Adella was leaving the stage forever, and like her alter ego, she knew she was blessed.

"I love you too," she whispered to the cheering crowd.

The curtain slowly lowered, and Adella took a deep breath, fighting the urge to sob. She wouldn't allow the others to see her pain.

Straightening her back, with her chin lifted high, she made her way into the wings. With the applause fading behind her, the shadows swallowed her proud form as the Diva walked away from the stage.

The End

My Prison

Raindrops pelted the aluminum siding, echoing through the emptiness inside. Thick black clouds blocked the sun, and wind rifled through the trees. Branches reached out with gnarled fingers to scrape on the windows, sending shrieks through the dark, forgotten rooms. The loose front door creaked open on rusted worn hinges, singing a silent song of sorrow.

This was my house.

Cobwebs wallpapered every corner, painting the walls a dingy brown with the collecting dust. Occasionally animals wandered inside for shelter. Rabbits, snakes, lizards, rats, mice, even a pair of raccoons who used their busy hands to unscrew the remaining knobs from the cabinets in the kitchen.

The open cupboards were bare except for the cracked remains of faded shelf lining. Warped linoleum covered the floor, the seams no longer joining together.

This was my house.

Wind poured through the broken glass at the end of the hall, blasting the worn window seat that used to overlook the flowers. How many days had I sat in that spot dreaming up fantastic tales? One day I might be a princess, and I would look out and see my Prince slaying a dragon for true love. Or if I were a singer, I would see an audience outside cheering and applauding me. If I was feeling lonely, I might picture myself as a wanderer from another planet. My imagination ran wild from my seat at the window. Shards of shattered glass were all that remained of the window now.

This was my house.

Stale air hung thick in my bedroom. Moth holes decorated the bedspread my mother made for me years ago. I lost count of how many. The embroidered outline of a little girl still remains, her button eyes stolen by animal visitors. The sunlight faded the rose color from her cheeks and lips, aging her timeless features, leaving behind a pale dusty ghost of who she once was.

I am that girl, and this was my room.

Trapped here in this web of memories, I'm lost in the present, and a prisoner of the past. I can see my home, but I cannot repair it. I can sing songs, but there is no music. I reach out, but I cannot touch. My spirit aches, but I feel no pain.

I don't know how long I've been here. I don't know how long I've been gone.

What will happen to me when the rain and wind finally reclaim these walls? When my house no longer stands, where will I go? Will I wander the wilderness? Will I be free or will I be lost?

I don't know what to wish for anymore. Despair has become my prince and loneliness my guardian.

As the rain turns to drizzle, the sun peers through the dark clouds. I can see the sunlight sparkling, dancing on the pond outside my shattered bedroom window. I fell in that pond once.

The light dazzled me on the smooth glass of the water. I reached out to touch it. The shock of the cold water still stings me when I remember falling in. The chill embraced me and pulled me under. I am not sure how long my body lay in the water before my parents found me.

I watched their sorrow, but I could not wipe

their tears.

They moved away after the accident. No one has been here since. The bushes have grown over the narrow dirt road that once led to this house. I wonder if anyone remembers it ever existed. I wonder if anyone cares. I cannot leave this place, and even death cannot save me now.

Death put me here.

This is my home.

This is my prison.

The End

The Chariot Race

The sun peered over the countryside, bathing the meadow and grazing horses in a warm orange glow. Arion's head shot up from the grass. He pranced, air under his hooves, head held high and proud, as puffs of steam shot out from his flared nostrils. He towered over the other equine, a vision. His proud neck arched up from his shoulder, giving him a regal aura of power.

Arion was the lead horse. Fierce with the other males, he accepted no challenges to his authority. Royal blood ran through every muscle, and his sleek coat glistened in the light of daybreak.

Only one chariot driver in Greece could command his free spirit.

She walked toward the large dapple grey stallion without fear, her dark eyes meeting his. Today they would make history. Today they would become legend. Immortality was within their grasp.

Cynisca stepped close to his chest, and he draped his muscular neck gently over her shoulder. Her tired fingers slid around his muzzle, gently rubbing at the secret spot underneath his chin making his upper lip quiver with pleasure. She bred this stallion and raised him from a foal for this day. She named him Arion after the legendary green-maned stallion Hercules rode when he seized Elis.

Arion was born from the Gods for speed.

She'd given her life to this team of horses, forsaking a husband and children. These horses were her children. Arion stood tall, the lead of her team, positioned on the left to pull them through the turns. Beside him ran Alexius, the most sure-footed of the team. He stabilized them if one should stumble. Next to him was her only mare, Elpis.

Elpis had a chestnut bay color coat, a stark contrast to the rest of the silver gray team. The mare matched Cynisca's braid that billowed behind her when they ran. She named Elpis, after the last spirit that remained in the jar after Pandora unleashed the evils. Elpis meant hope. The mare ran with all of her heart, just as Cynisca did.

They would be the only two females in the hippodrome on this day.

And finally, Aniketos flanked the team at the far right. His spirit matched his name, meaning unconquerable. She smiled watching him graze in the shadows. Aniketos was still an unbroken stallion. No one could ride on his back, but once he was harnessed with the team, he ran like the wind itself.

No one knew better than Cynisca. She trained them herself for this race.

"This is our day Arion," she cooed. "Today we leave our mark on Olympia." Her gaze moved from the horses to the ornately carved chariot at the edge of the meadow as she whispered, "Today we win."

Victory was no stranger to Cynisca. Four years before, her horses won the tethrippon in the main stadium of the Olympics.

But she had not witnessed their victory.

Women were forbidden to participate in the Olympics. In fact, they were not even allowed to watch the games. So while she was recognized and honored as the first woman in history to win at the Olympic Games, her feet hadn't touched the dust inside the stadium.

Her eyes narrowed as she stared at the chariot. This time would be different.

She was the first woman to breed chariot horses, then she became the first to train them, but today she would gain a new first.

Today she would be the first woman to hold the reins and drive her own team of horses in the deadly race.

Stroking his muzzle one last time, Cynisca stepped away from Arion. There was still so much to do. She clenched and straightened her sore aching fingers, hoping to stretch the exhausted tendons.

Holding the reins of four racing horses while guiding them through the gauntlet of competitors was tough for any man, and she was two feet shorter than most of the other drivers. Her shoulders were tight, and pain radiated down her back, but she held her head high, not allowing the suffering to show on her face or in her stature.

The other drivers would not see her weakness now. Not when she was so close to her dream.

She tucked her long thick braid of chestnut brown hair inside her tunic to keep it out of the way while she knelt down to examine the wheels of her chariot. One crack could lead to a shattered wheel in a turn, which could equal death to the drivers and horses.

Satisfied that her wheels were intact, she lay on the moist grass under the chariot and inspected the axle underneath. Her brow furrowed as she focused on the task at hand. Everything seemed in order, and yet fear was a shadow over her heart. The quiet moments allowed dread and worry to stalk her, enticing her to question her decisions.

What was she trying to prove by risking her life and the lives of her beloved horses? She had already won once.

Puffing out a sigh of frustration, she dragged herself out from under the chariot. Fear would not command her heart. She was the daughter of a Spartan King. She trained and owned the swiftest chariot team in all of Olympia, and by the Gods in Olympus, she would hold the reins in this race.

And she would win.

Her slave boy, Petros, hustled to her chariot with woven mats and blankets to wipe down the horses before the grand procession into the hippodrome.

"Remember, I will bring Arion in from the field," she said as he passed by.

"It will be done." He kept his eyes downcast from her face.

Cynisca started to smile. "Thank you, Petros."

He peered up at her from under his brow with a conspiratorial grin, and winked before hustling off into the field to bring the other horses in.

She and Petros didn't share a traditional slave and master relationship. Petros was her only real friend, but in these situations, they needed to keep their friendship hidden, lest he be beaten as a disorderly slave.

It was an unkind world.

Cynisca entered her tent and found Petros had laid out her new linens for the race. Unlike the other games of the Olympiad in which the athletes competed in the games naked, during the chariot race full length togas were worn to protect the drivers from dirt and rocks thrown up from the horses hooves.

She used a colorful sash to cinch the toga down and keep it close to her body, eliminating the billowing of the fabric. Should a stray bit of fabric get tangled in the axle of a passing chariot, the driver could be yanked from his own chariot.

She cinched hers a little tighter and stepped back outside.

Chariots and teams of horses already gathered along the dirt road leading to the hippodrome. Cynisca shifted her shoulders, trying to loosen her taunt muscles, then raised her chin and started toward her chariot with a confident stride. Petros awaited with Alexius, Elpis and Aniketos already harnessed and bridled. He met her eyes for a brief moment as she approached.

"Your horses are ready."

"Thank you Petros." She picked up Arion's bridle and kept her expression stoic as she offered a forbidden compliment under her breath. "I could not attempt this without your help."

He smiled and lowered his eyes before any of the others noticed his forward behavior. "I am honored to assist you. Today will be a day that lives on in song and story."

"Let us hope," she whispered.

Cynisca walked into the field and called out to Arion. His powerful neck arched up, and his ears pricked forward when he heard her voice. With an even gait he trotted toward her, stretching his muscled haunches.

The summer breeze blew back through his silver mane and tail as he moved, and in spite of her attempt to remain solemn, a smile crept to the corners of her full lips. Arion was a vision of grace and power. He was ready for this race.

Was she?

The stallion lowered his head, taking the bit into his mouth as she slid the crown piece over his ears. Petros was close by fitting the harness around him and wiping his coat with the grooming cloth. Cynisca brought Arion to his position on the left side beside Alexius.

While Petros fastened the chariot to the

final harness she addressed the sleek beasts that she had raised and trained since birth. Their dark eyes never left her face, watching her with the intensity of any human athlete. Over the years, she had found horses to be incredible listeners, and they kept secrets better than any human being on the earth.

"Today is our day, our victory. Today we run in the contest of men, and we will rise above them. May the Gods watch over us and give my arms the strength to guide you, and may you find sure footing, and fast strides. My friends, today we will taste immortality."

She placed a kiss to each muzzle before stepping to the back of the chariot. Petros handed her the reins, four for each hand. She laced the worn leather through her sore, calloused fingers. With a deep breath, she clenched the reins and stepped up into the chariot.

"May the Gods be with you, Cynisca," Petros said.

She bowed her head for a moment, calling to Nike, the Goddess of strength, speed and victory. "Watch over my team beloved Goddess. May the horses be swift and their hooves sure. Today you can raise this woman above the men of Olympia. Praise be to you Goddess."

She opened her eyes and lifted her head, her face a mask of determination, her chin tilted up slightly in defiance. She had no use for fear.

Not this day.

With a cluck of her tongue, her team came to life, prancing in a slow gate as she guided them forward to the hippodrome. Horns announced their arrival as they entered the large stadium.

Thousands of men lined the ring, their cheers echoing and mingling with the horns until they became one deafening noise.

Her team tugged at the reins, and Arion let out a fiery snort from his nostrils. Cynisca leaned back, holding the horses in check with her weight. They needed to complete one lap around the stadium to their respective starting position.

She couldn't let them run yet.

The sun beat down on the chariots. Sweat trickled down her back as she waited for the starting call. Elpis shifted her weight in anticipation; sweaty foam already traced the edge of the harness. The large animals could sense the tension, and they were ready.

Silence washed over the crowd. She kept her eyes forward, fighting the urge to look to the side to watch for the official to call out the signal. Holding her focus on the chariots in her line of sight, Cynisca held tight to the reins.

When the starting call pealed she didn't hesitate, raising her right hand she brought the reins down hard over Arion's haunches.

"Ha!" she screamed. Sand and gravel flew up, pelting her face as her team leapt forward, their hooves digging into the earth with every stride.

The hippodrome erupted with cheers, as her horses built speed. The hot wind stung her face. She squinted, struggling to see through the thick dust and maneuver her horses around her competitors.

The other drivers were young, barely men at all. Each chariot owner sought out the lightest framed man to drive his team so that the horses were not pulling much weight behind them. The only requirement for the young men was to be strong enough to grasp eight reins and hold the massive animals together in the tight corners, or risk their chariot turning over.

Crashes were commonplace in the races. Deaths were frequent.

Sweat soaked through her tunic between her shoulder blades as Cynisca leaned into the first turn. Pulling back with her left hand while lengthening her reins in the right, she guided her team with smooth precision.

As she rounded out of the first turn, screams burst out behind her and the crack of splintering wood echoed over the howling crowd of spectators.

She risked a quick glance over her shoulder, and winced at the tangled mass of carnage. Two chariots had collided, throwing the drivers out onto the track. There was no way to stop the horses now. The rumble of hoof beats muffled as teams trampled over the bodies in a frenzy for the finish. Her jaw clenched; her brow furrowed.

Concentrate or her fate could be the same.

Cynisca encouraged Arion faster, and he drove the team to stretch out their strides. Only one chariot remained in front of her, and only one lap was left to make history.

As she came up on the outside of the final turn, she pushed her team even faster, fighting to pass the black chariot drawn by four black stallions. Once again she leaned into the turn, only to find the other driver pulling to the right, widening his turn to cut her off.

"This is not a woman's place!" The driver screamed.

She didn't offer an answer. Not with words.

Instead, Cynisca bent her knees, crouching down into the base of her chariot. Grabbing the edge of the wood with her right hand, she held tight, and then yanked on the reins in her left hand with all of the strength that remained in her body.

Her team veered sharply to the left, and passed the black chariot on the inside. The right wheel lifted off the ground and she held her breath, sending a silent plea to the Gods to keep her chariot from flipping over.

The left wheel creaked. Cynisca straightened and leaned to the right as they entered the final straight of the track. Her weight shifted the chariot back onto both wheels as the horses galloped with reckless abandon.

The finish was in sight.

Cynisca stretched her hands forward, giving her horses free rein to run. Peering back over her shoulder, she could see the black chariot following her, the driver whipping his team. She faced forward again, keeping her eyes on the finish.

"Ha!" She called out to her team. They responded with a final burst of speed that propelled them past the finish line.

Cynisca screamed as she hauled back on the reins, fighting to regain control over the sixteen powerful legs in front of her. When they finally slowed to a trot, Petros appeared at the sidelines, racing to catch Arion's bridle.

With the team stopped, Cynisca slowly turned toward the crowd, not sure if they would ridicule or cheer her victory.

Her heart pounded, her fingers bled, rubbed raw by the leather of the reins, and tears ran down her dusty cheeks as she scanned the crowd.

Every man was on his feet, clapping and cheering her name as if they were all one voice.

A woman had just won the chariot race.

She stepped away from the wheeled cart and approached the podium to acknowledge the crowd. Her eyes darted over to her beautiful horses, their nostrils still flared and red, then to her only true friend, Petros.

He smiled openly up at her, and she felt a new wave of proud tears slip from her eyes.

Cynisca raised her exhausted arms and announced in full voice. "Kings of Sparta were my forefathers and my brothers. I assert that I am the only woman in all of Greece who has won this crown."

The crowd roared as she lowered her head and accepted her laurel wreath.

And her immortality.

The End

Cynisca won the Olympic tethrippon, the four horse chariot race, in 396BC and 392 BC, paving the way for more women to compete.

A bronze statue was erected in Cynisca's honor to memorialize her accomplishment. Over the centuries, the statue deteriorated, but the base still remains to this day at the ancient site of the first Olympics. The inscription still reads:

> *"Kings of Sparta were my forefathers and my brothers. Victorious Cynisca with her chariot drawn by swift-footed horses erected this statue. I assert that I am the only woman in all Greece who has won this crown."*

A Demon on the Drums

Strobe lights flashed, freezing the crowd for a split second. Frame by frame he watched bodies writhe to the driving beat of the drums. The electric guitars wailed, drowning out the screams of sweaty voyeurs below.

The mosh pit was chaos. The air reeked of sweat and beer. Hash smoke mingled with the manufactured fog while the band fed the crowd's frenzy. He scanned the mob with a slow sweep of his yellow eyes.

"Whoa! Cool contacts, Dude!" An inebriated human screamed as he passed by.

With just a thought, he slammed the man against the concrete wall and grinned when the unconscious body slid to the floor in a heap.

It would have been more delicious to kill him, but he'd found over the centuries that killing mortals with large crowds of witnesses only led to more work, and lately he'd been less into working and more into his new passion.

His drum set.

Since the dawn of time, Apep had been the God of Evil. The Egyptians immortalized him as a snake and dubbed him the Serpent of the Nile. His name meant "spat out" and quite literally, he was thrust into the mortal world because none of the immortal worlds wanted him. He was the enemy of Ra, and any object or deity that represented light and goodness.

He used to get off on his own bad-ass reputation. Just the thought of torturing mortals, and hearing their pleas and screams used to make him salivate.

Used to.

That was a long time ago.

Six thousand years later, he remained, still trapped on this human plane. But mortals no longer feared him. Today he was simply a footnote in history. Mankind had forgotten him. Humans didn't need a demon with reptilian eyes to frighten them anymore. They had horror movies with Freddy and Jason to lurk in the shadows and haunt their dreams.

He didn't give a shit anyway.

He lost interest in humans nearly two thousand years ago. They were too easy to kill, and their lives were too short to even befriend the wicked ones. It left him alone to entertain himself with mischief. Tsunamis were his current disaster du jour, but even watching a tidal wave of water destroy entire cities only held his interest for a few years.

Music was different.

It started with Sympathy for the Devil.

Not that he had any.

No, he recently attended a Rolling Stones concert. At the time, he'd had his reptilian eyes focused on Keith Richards, but honestly, which demon didn't?

His plan was to possess the ancient rocker and spend a few years experiencing the world as a rock star. He stole a front row ticket from an unsuspecting couple, and had to admit, it still gave him a little jolt of excitement to watch a couple fight when they thought they lost something that he had actually stolen from them. Delicious.

He never dreamed that he would be the one to be possessed that night.

Mick Jagger strutted across the stage and looked directly into Apep's eyes as he sang "Pleased to meet you, won't you guess my name..."

And from that moment, Apep wanted to be a rock star. He didn't want to possess a rock star.

Not anymore. He wanted to *be* a rock star. He wanted to perform on a stage with thousands of people chanting his name.

He wanted to be worshiped again.

Soon he had a guitar, but between his inhuman strength and his razor sharp nails, it was nearly impossible for him to play without breaking the fine metal electric guitar strings.

Singing lead vocals was even more difficult. With his forked tongue, he rasped out rock lyrics with a lisp. Not worthy of worship.

But the drums were different.

First off, he liked that the stool was referred to as a throne. Fitting for a God. Secondly, he was the leader of the band. Sure he wasn't strutting out front like Mick Jagger, but every song depended on him for the tempo. He was in charge. He was the beat, the pulse of the song.

He could hit the toms, but hit was an understatement. He could wail on them, while pounding the bass drum with the foot petal. All of his frustrations, all of his passion and anger and rage and hate pulsed through each song. With a crash of the cymbal and a furious drum roll on the snare, he could be nature's thunder. He could scream fire into the souls of men again.

Now that made his mouth water.

So did ABBA.

That's what brought him to Biff's Bar

tonight. He came to pass the night away with AbbaCadabra. And to replace their drummer.

Or kill him. Apep was happy to do whatever was necessary.

This UK band combined the catchy ABBA tunes he secretly enjoyed, with the grit and rage of heavy metal, racing drum beats, and shrieking guitars in contrast with fearless female vocals. He had to hear it for himself, and they were better than he imagined. The set opened with a loud, driving version of Voulez Vous that sent his demon blood racing. It was glorious. Each song they played made him ache to be on stage to answer his new calling in this world.

He was ready.

Apep drank in the noise from the band and the roar of the crowd as he made his way toward the stage. Two men in the corner carefully straightened lines of cocaine on a cocktail napkin as he passed by, and with a thought and a quick flick of his forked tongue, the cocaine transformed into BC headache powder. Behind him he heard the men gasp and cough, retching, while one of them screamed in pain.

BC powder burned.

Apep smiled and kept moving. Torturing mortals at random still brought him pleasure. He couldn't help it. They were so easy.

When he reached the stage, his eyes

narrowed, watching the drummer. The light reflected off the bass drum as he pounded the tempo with his foot and his hands danced across the toms and the cymbal. He never missed a beat, or a division of the beat.

Apep frowned, glaring at the man on the throne. He wanted to see flaws, to hear inconsistencies with the tempo.

Instead he caught himself enjoying it. The drummer wasn't flashy, no tossing of the drumsticks, or crossing hands, but he closed his eyes and instinctively knew where each drum head was located. He felt it.

And Apep was torn.

He was beginning to tolerate the human. Strange.

They started their final song, Knowing Me, Knowing You. His favorite ABBA song.

Apep watched as the lead guitar started, followed by a second guitar, and finally the drums entered with an urgent tempo, demanding the listener to come along for the wild ride.

The crowd cheered, a dancing mob of humanity. Every slam of the cymbals called to Apep's inner demon. This was his song like he had never heard it before.

And when the final cymbal crash broke the spell, Apep applauded along with the rest of the humans.

The band left the stage, and Apep stared at the empty drum set. It would be nothing to kill the drummer and take his position in the band. No one would suspect while he helped the band through the tragedy.

Apep paused, pondering his future, and without a word turned and walked out.

He would steal their CDs on the way, but wouldn't be a part of their band.

The drummer's playing had saved his own life.

Apep's boot heels clicked along the pavement. He snatched his sticks from the pocket inside of his trench coat and spun them around each knuckle in agitation. A wail of electric guitars erupted from another club across the street, and his lips curled into an evil smile.

Their drummer would not be so lucky.

The End

Internet Dating Secrets

She stormed out of the restaurant and down the sidewalk, yanking her jacket around as she jammed her other arm inside the sleeve. She knew agreeing to a date with someone she met over the internet would be a disaster, but no, her friends had all tried it and said it was fun.

Well not tonight.

Todd had seemed like her perfect match on the Komodo Island music message boards. They both enjoyed the same bands. He seemed funny and intelligent. Plus, they'd already been emailing for a few weeks. She felt like she knew him.

Apparently it's tough to judge a person's character on a message board.

"Wait! Janet, wait up!"

With a drop-dead-you-jerk groan, she struggled to walk even faster, but in spite of her speed, he caught up and matched her stride.

"Please, let me explain."

She stopped on a dime and glared up at him. "Look Todd, this was our second date. There's no need to explain anything. We don't have a relationship, so it's fine. I get it."

"No, you really don't. Not quite all of it."

He had gorgeous eyes. She had to give him that. But arriving at the restaurant only to find him cozying up with a tall blonde in a short black skirt was too much. At least she found out what kind of guy he really was before she invested too much time in the relationship.

"Enough. You don't need to explain anything to me," she said. "I saw it for myself. What I don't understand is if you weren't interested in me, why did you ask me out? Did you think it would be fun to embarrass me?"

"No, that was never my intention. I..."

"Well you did." She rolled her eyes. "I don't know why I'm even talking to you."

"She's not what you..."

"Oh please! Don't tell me it's not what it looks like."

His jaw clenched. "If you'd quit interrupting me, then I could explain."

"Fine." Janet crossed her arms. "Go ahead."

He looked down the street and took a slow, deep breath. As he exhaled, the crisp night air turned his breath into a soft cloud of fog. Waiting for him to dream up a great lie was driving her nuts.

Janet glanced toward the traffic light, following his gaze, and frowned. The streets were empty. No cars passed by, no sounds of people talking or dogs barking. Where was everyone? The quiet surrounding them was almost palpable.

Weird, she thought to herself as she ran her hands up and down her arms. Looking back up at Todd, a chill shot down her spine. The fog from his breath was taking shape. Shifting.

"How did you..."

"Shhh... I've got to concentrate," he whispered.

Gradually he lifted his hand, his fingers tapping out an invisible melody in the air. Her jaw dropped when she heard the faint cry of a single guitar. Where was the music coming from? The fog dipped until it looked like a small staircase, and finally she recognized the tune.

"It's Stairway to Heaven." She glanced back up at him. "How..."

Sweat beaded on his brow as his hand lowered back to his side and his eyes met hers. "I told you I was a Mage."

"Yeah but," she watched the stairs drift away into the night. "I thought you meant you were a computer gamer. You know, World of Warcraft or Ever Quest or... something."

He shook his head with a hint of a smile. "Nope. I'm the real thing."

Janet stared down the street. Noise encroached on the silence as the magic disappeared with the music. It couldn't be real. Could it?

Todd took her hand in his. "I'm sorry if I scared you, but I wasn't sure you'd believe me if I didn't show you."

"I'm not sure I believe even after you showed me..." Her words faded as she gave his hand a squeeze. "Your hand is like ice."

"It takes a lot out of me to channel that much magic all at once. I'm still in training."

Right on cue, the tall, leggy blonde applauded and walked toward them. Todd stepped back with a smile. "Janet, I'd like you to meet Aria Dobson. I'm her apprentice."

"Apprentice?" Janet asked, as she shook hands with Aria. "So you're his..."

"Mentor," she answered. "Not his date. Sorry about the confusion."

Janet blushed with a shrug. "That's ok. I guess I was jumping to conclusions, but in my defense, who would have ever believed..."

Aria laughed. "That he's magic? There are

believers out there. Sometimes you just have to," she glanced at Todd. "Open their eyes."

With a crooked smirk, she snapped her fingers, leaving only echo behind.

Todd caught Janet's hand and placed it in the crook of his arm. "So, can we start over?"

She grinned. "You just made time stand still to serenade me with my favorite song. I suppose I could let you buy me dinner."

"Good. Oh and Janet?"

"Yes?"

"You can't tell anyone about this."

She chuckled as she stepped through the door into the restaurant. "Who would believe me?"

Todd led her to the booth, and Janet picked up her menu with a smile. She had a secret to share too.

Just wait until the next full moon...

The End

The Bet

The safest road to hell is the gradual one - the gentle slope, soft underfoot, without sudden turnings, without milestones, without signposts. – C.S. Lewis

Strange things happen in the Walmart parking lot after midnight.

Late Sunday nights were Jarod's favorite shift. The parking lot emptied earlier than other nights and usually stayed pretty deserted. Maybe the Walmart shoppers were all home getting ready for the new work week. He liked to imagine their lives. Some of them were probably doctors, maybe some garbage collectors, teachers, spies, witches, werewolves, ok so maybe not many werewolves, but you never knew, right?

The cool night air blew his hair back as he

rode the runaway shopping cart through the shadowed northwest corner of the parking lot. Jarod was tall and lanky, probably six feet in his socks. Standing up on the back of the cart, he easily gained another six inches. His reflective vest flapped in the breeze. He pictured himself on the racetrack, leaning into the final turn of the Indy 500.

"And Landers heads into the final turn with the lead. The crowd goes wild! Yeeeeeeeaaaahhhh!"

He had the best imaginary fans.

As he approached the bank of carts he'd already pressed into a tight line, one of the plastic wheels in the front started shuddering in a death wobble and the cart careened out of control. Jarod ejected and watched it smash into the orderly line.

"Landers goes down in flames! Medics are on the track." He grabbed the handle and pulled the cart back before stuffing it into the ever growing line.

Once he had the cart contained, he gave the entire line a push, urging the wheeled mass forward toward the distant glow of the superstore.

"The end is coming."

Jarod stopped pushing and spun around toward the shadows to see an elderly man leaning against the last light post in the corner of the lot.

The yellow overhead light sucked all the

color from the man standing underneath it, like a monotone figure from an old black and white television screen. Jarod could hear the Twilight Zone theme in his head and Rod Serling warning him that he'd just crossed over. Creepy.

"Can I help you, sir?" Jarod asked.

The old man shook his head. "No, but I can help you. Are you ready for the rapture, son?"

"Rapture?" Jarod's internal soundtrack started playing Blondie. He couldn't help it.

"Yes, the end of the world," the old man said. "It's coming soon. Is your soul prepared?"

"How do you know the world's ending?" Jarod asked.

The old man smiled, and the yellow light overhead cast long shadows along every wrinkle. Jarod tried not to shrink back, but it wasn't a pretty sight.

"Mules can reproduce."

"What?"

"Mules," the old man repeated. "Mankind created the mule, and now they can reproduce. Do you understand what that means, son?"

Jarod had no clue what the old man was talking about, but he figured he could humor the old-timer. It would fall under customer service as far as he was concerned. "Mules are gonna destroy the world?"

"No, no! Not mules. The world is

changing because of mankind, don't you see?"

The old man heaved a sigh. Apparently the old guy could tell that he couldn't see. Not at all.

"It's like this young man, when mankind crossed species by breeding horses and donkeys together, they created a whole new animal, the mule. Because mules were an unnatural species, they were born infertile. They were a man-made creation. But now there are mules who can conceive! They've evolved!" He waved his bony hands around to illustrate his point. "Mankind is playing God and when the time comes man will have to face His wrath."

"Over mules?"

"Not mules, Boy! Over playing God. What do you think these scientists are doing when they make clones and new species of unnatural animals?"

Jarod struggled to make sense of the crazy old man, but his customer service training didn't cover this type of interaction. He glanced back over his shoulder at the store, hoping the codger would take the hint.

"God will punish mankind. You'll see!" Some spittle flew off his bottom lip. "So is your soul prepared for the end?"

Jarod shrugged. "I guess so. Look, I've gotta get these carts back."

The old man lurched toward him. "Your

immortal soul is worth more than minimum wage, boy."

"Maybe so, but my soul still needs to pay rent this month." Jarod took a step back toward the carts, telling himself it was because he needed to work, not because he wanted to get further away from the wrinkled-black-and-white-television man.

The old guy tipped his head back and laughed, exposing what few teeth he had left, but when his laughter died away; his eyes almost glowed with intensity. Jarod glanced up at the light post. It had to be the lighting. The hunched, wrinkled man lumbered forward another step. His gaze kept Jarod frozen where he stood.

"I like the way you think... What's your name, boy?"

Before Jarod could respond, another person stepped out from the shadows. "Don't tell him!"

Jarod turned to find a stout old woman at least a foot shorter than him waddling closer to them.

"He wants your name so he can take your soul."

"What?" Jarod's face contorted with confusion. Was she nuts? "What are you talking about?"

The old man glared at the little round woman and spat. "We were having a private conversation. No one invited you."

"As I saw it, no one invited *you*. This young man was just doing his honest job for his honest pay. He never invited you here."

"This is public property woman," the old man grunted. "I can be here same as you."

Jarod watched their exchange back and forth like he was watching the final match at Wimbledon.

"You have no business with this boy. You leave him be." She gave a stern nod that further punctuated her command.

"I asked the boy for his name, not his soul."

"Yet," she countered back.

Jarod was getting whiplash. "Sorry to break this up, but I've really gotta get these carts back inside."

They both stared at Jarod. The old man frowned which caused almost as many shadow wrinkles as his smile did. At the same time the old woman wore a serene Mona Lisa smile. Under the yellow lights, they both gave him the creeps.

"You can go back inside, dear," she said. "We'll settle this ourselves."

Jarod stared from one to the other. Something was definitely not right, but either way, he didn't feel good about leaving an old woman alone in a parking lot after midnight. His Mom raised him better than that.

"Look it's really late. Can I walk you to

your cars?" Jarod looked around and noticed for the first time that there wasn't another car in the front lot. Not one. "Hey, how did you two get here?"

The old man's eyes sparkled again as he turned toward the round woman. His smile quirked to the side, contorting the shadow wrinkles until he looked... Wicked.

"You gonna tell him?"

Her smile melted away as she looked up at Jarod. "Don't mind him. Just go on about your work. We'll be fine."

Jarod looked at the blazing Walmart light and wished he could just go back to work. Fog billowed around them and a chill shot down Jarod's back. "It's getting cold out. Why don't you guys come inside with me. We have a phone you can use to call a ride."

"Thank you for your kindness," the old man said as he offered out a bony hand. "I'm Jeb by the way."

Jarod shook his hand, surprised by how warm it felt, almost hot. "Hi Jeb, I'm–"

"Not so fast boy." The old woman shook a finger at him. "Remember what I told you about sharing your name. You don't want Jeb here having that kind of power over you."

"Oh stop interferin' you old witch," he grumbled, yanking his hand back.

Jarod looked from one to the other, scratching his head. "I don't get you two. Jeb was out here trying to save my soul because mules can have babies, and then you show up telling me not to give him my name like it's some sort of magic word. Neither one of you makes any sense."

The stout old woman stepped toward him, lowering her voice as if she had the winning lottery numbers to share with him. "The dark powers that lurk in the shadows don't always come in the forms you would expect."

"A dark power?" He glanced from one senior citizen to the other and shrugged his thin shoulders. "I'm sorry but I better get these carts in before my manager gets upset with me. Are you sure you don't want me to call you a cab?"

The fogeys chuckled and shook their heads in unison.

"Fine," Jarod said, moving up to the line of carts. "Have a nice night then."

He leaned all his body weight against the long trail of carts and gradually got them rolling back toward the store. He couldn't help glancing back over his shoulder when he overheard them talking behind him.

"You owe me, Jeb. I told you that boy's soul wasn't for you."

"It woulda been if you weren't interfering."

"Ha! You think you were winning him

over with the mule story?"

"It was workin'."

"Yeah right. Stop being a sore loser. You owe me a Frappuccino from Starbucks. Just pay up."

Jarod frowned as he made his way to the front doors and shoved the carts through to Brian, who guided them inside. Looking back out at the parking lot, Jarod's eyes widened. He rubbed them and shook his head.

Did Jeb really have a... Tail? And the old woman had something on her back. Some things. Wings? He flinched when Brian stepped up and placed a hand on his shoulder.

"You okay man? You look like you just saw a ghost or something."

"Or something..." Jarod nodded.

Brian shrugged. "I told you the late shift was freaky..." He pointed at the old folks walking away. "So who are they?"

"I'm not sure." Jarod watched them disappear into the shadows before he looked back at Brian again. "But I think they just bet my soul to see who pays for Starbucks."

Strange things happen in the Walmart parking lot after midnight.

The End

Going Home

"Lieutenant Briggs, report back. Briggs?" Pause. "Answer me, Briggs."

The lieutenant dialed down the volume on his ear piece, and walked away from the pod into the wasteland that was once his home planet. Dust plumed around his white boots with every step.

He hadn't expected to feel this way.

His mission was simple enough. Return to the home planet and retrieve historical documents. Books to be exact. He wasn't quite sure what a real book looked like. The world population hadn't used them for centuries. He couldn't imagine what life before the internet could have been like. The internet itself seemed like an archaic concept.

Centuries ago, the human world came together through the antiquated form of communication, but as technology improved, computers gave way to handheld devices, and voice-recognition software led to the extinction of the keyboard, until technology and mankind existed as one unified race.

Briggs stared down the deserted twelve lane highway. The red laser lights shot up from the pavement, designating the flight lanes for civilian air traffic as if the rush hour of personal spacecraft might flood the area any moment.

There hadn't been any traffic on this stretch of highway in over one hundred years.

His heartbeat was the only sound left on the empty planet. A chill shot down his spine.

Briggs cranked up the volume on his earpiece, grateful for the noise to break through the suffocating silence.

"Briggs... Report in. That's an order."

He pressed a button on his belt. "I'm here commander. Just getting my bearings back, Sir." A century had come and gone since he'd been on the surface.

His commanding officer let out a sigh of relief. "Jesus man, we thought we lost you. Do you see your target?"

Briggs pressed a button on the control pad of his left wrist, lowering his long-range goggles inside of his helmet. According to his readout, the large stone building was just over a mile away.

"My target is in sight, Commander."

"Good. Radio back when you're at the final destination."

"Yes sir."

He dialed down the volume and pressed the button to retract the goggles. After the computer verified his fuel levels and completed the flight safety check, he clicked a button on his wrist and rose up off of the sand-covered concrete of the abandoned highway.

Careful to maintain a slow speed while remaining close to the surface, he made his way toward the World Library of Congress building.

Wind gusts tugged at his flight suit and threw ancient bits of frozen garbage around his head. The temperature outside of his suit registered seventy below zero, fairly typical for a mid-summer's night. Since the man-made atmosphere had failed, it was impossible to maintain sustainable temperatures for humans. The planet was evacuated after his first lifetime following his full organ replacement.

He passed an old McDonald's sign; proudly proclaiming billions and billions served and chuckled. Could the founders have ever dreamed that the Big Mac would outlive the cockroach? The signature burgers were still available on their new space station. Cockroaches went extinct when the atmosphere dome cracked.

He looked past the faded sign and saw only remnants of the once stylish fast-food building. Space had claimed most of it now. Only part of one wall and the foundation remained.

His stomach growled, yanking him from his trip down memory lane. He had a mission to accomplish.

Only it wasn't the mission the federation sent him to complete.

Briggs made his way toward the world library of congress building, but two blocks before he reached the grand structure, he turned right down a lonely side street. With a click on the control pad on his wrist, the jet boosters in his suit quieted and his feet came to rest on the frigid pavement.

He would walk the final block.

Empty buildings watched him pass, staring down at the intruder in their silent world. Gusts of cold air slammed into him, but his climate-controlled suit fought off the attack. He hadn't been home in over a century, yet he could still make this solemn trek without the aid of his computer's mapping system.

When he rounded the corner, his eyes widened.

The cemetery was no longer a soft carpet of

green grass, but a barren wasteland of sand. Some of the larger headstones rose up from the turbulent sand storms dancing around them. He struggled to orient himself and remember the layout of the once restful place he used to visit every week. The rows and columns of the cemetery were now nonexistent, and his heart pounded with anxiety.

How would he ever find her again?

"Heart rate is elevated. Are you in distress?" His computer queried.

"Stable," he answered and punched the button to disable the vital sign monitor.

He made his way toward what remained of a large granite angel. A century of furious sand storms had taken their toll on her now featureless face. Without eyes or a nose or mouth, she was a blank canvas marking the resting place of a small child. He turned around and started counting his paces. She had been buried three rows south of the angel.

He could only guess at the distance.

After counting thirty paces he slowed and knelt on the ground. Reaching out his gloved hands, he dusted away the sand, wrestling against time itself to find her. Sand plumed, flying up around him. He finally brushed across something solid. A marker, but not the one he was searching for.

"Dammit!"

He shifted to the right and started the process all over again until he finally found the words he'd been seeking.

Harmony Briggs, beloved wife and best friend. Gone too soon.

"I miss you, Harm." His eyes brimmed with tears as his fingers traced the engraving of her name. "I never should have left you here."

He tipped his head up, fighting to blink back the tears. It was impossible to wipe his eyes inside of his climate-control suit. After a century apart, he thought he'd have better control over his emotions, but seeing her resting place now, desolate. It was more than he could bear. He left her in a barren desert, a wasteland, forgotten along with the rest of the dead.

Briggs sighed and looked back down at her name as a single tear spilled down his cheek. "I didn't know it would be like this."

He laid down alongside her burial place wishing he could feel the cold stone, just to know he was closer to her. Instead he settled for resting his gloved hand over her name. "When we left the planet, I thought we'd be coming home eventually. This was the first assignment I could get that brought me back to you."

He shared stories of deep space and black holes, meetings with new races from other galaxies. He'd never remarried after Harmony's organ replacement had failed. Without any children, he outlived his family and was painfully aware he was alone in the universe.

Not anymore.

After a couple of hours, he vaguely registered his computer warning light. Oxygen levels were running low. His commanding officer was probably urging him to answer and open radio communications, but he hadn't come back home to retrieve the ancient books for the Federation. Not really.

He came back to be with Harmony.

He had no intention of leaving her now.

His breath was shallow, and his face shone with a thin layer of perspiration. He rolled onto his back and stared up at the stars. High above, he could see the outline of a brown planet, surrounded by a haze of gases.

Earth. The first forgotten planet.

He'd never been on Earth. Mars was the only planet he'd ever called home. He closed his eyes and exhaled his last breath. Somewhere in the recesses of his mind he heard her voice calling to him. His lips curved as his heart fluttered and finally went still.

"Welcome Home, Briggs. I missed you too."

The End

Desert Storm

Hot desert wind blew through her long blond hair, snapping it behind her like a whip. She glanced down at the temperature gauge on her old banana yellow VW Bug, watching it inch up toward the red.

"Come on Baby you can make it," she murmured to her car.

Lightning arced across the sky, throwing the shadow of her car onto the deserted highway in front of her. Brianna gasped, her gaze moving to the rearview mirror. The clouds churned, racing up behind her. Another bolt of electricity sizzled through the night, and a crack of thunder echoed across the empty valley.

Death Valley.

She gripped the steering wheel a little tighter and pressed the accelerator to the floor. The drive back from Las Vegas was a nail-biter. The hot, dry desert air was always ripe for electrical storms, but with the storms often came hail and torrential rain. Since the cloth top of her 1964 Beetle convertible was currently stuck in the down position, come-hell-or-high-water she needed to stay ahead of the dark clouds brewing behind her.

Another rumble of thunder bellowed across the desert. It was getting closer. She checked the rearview mirror again, only darkness followed her now. Even the moon was hidden behind the storm's fury.

She heaved a sigh and concentrated on the highway ahead of her. The empty highway. Her lips pressed together. Although the drive across the Mojave Desert was desolate, there were usually other cars sharing the highway.

But not tonight. Weird.

Reaching over to twist the knob on her radio, she almost smiled when K-Earth 101 blared through the speakers.

"As we live a life of ease, every one of us has all we need..."

"All we need," she sang into the wind.

"Sky of blue and sea of green. In our yellow

submarine."

"Ah-ha!" She started to smile in spite of the impending downpour.

"God, Bri, I'm trying to sleep."

She rolled her eyes and glanced over at her bleary-eyed boyfriend. "Oh sure, you can sleep through the wrath-of-God lightning and thunder, but I sing the Beatles and it wakes you up."

"Guess so." He chuckled and sat up. Strands of blinding light suddenly cut through the darkness over them, followed by a deafening clap of thunder. "Wow!"

"Yeah." She checked the rearview mirror again and pressed her foot to the floor. "I don't know if I'll be able to outrun the storm."

He turned around. "It looks nasty back there."

"I just got these seats replaced and the radio restored." She gripped the wheel tighter like that might make her VW bug go faster. "I can't let everything get wet!"

"Damn." He faced forward again. "I should've bought a tarp when we found out the convertible top was stuck."

"It's not your fault, Brad. We're in the desert. It's not like rain is the first thing you'd think would..." Her voice trailed off as the sky lit up with an orange glow.

Streaks of orange and yellow alternated in

the darkness overhead. Brad looked up as Brianna fought to keep her attention on the road.

"What is that?"

"I don't know," he said. "Maybe a meteor shower or something?"

"A meteor shower? Can we see those without a telescope?"

Brad shook his head without taking his eyes off the strange light show. "I don't know. I'm just guessing."

The bright light gradually faded away, and Brianna cranked up the radio. "Oh I love this song!"

Major Tom blared out her speakers.

"4 3 2 1
Earth below us
drifting falling
floating weightless
calling, calling home..."

Her hair blew across her face as she sang along. She reached up with one hand to brush it back behind her ear, when Brad turned the radio off.

"Hey, why'd you do—"

"Pull over Bri."

"What? But the storm--"

"Just do it!" He yelled. "Pull over now."

She turned on her blinker and moved across the lanes of the highway. When the VW finally stopped on the shoulder, she looked over at Brad. "What's going on?"

"Just come with me."

"Where?" She scanned the desert around the car. "We can't just leave my car here."

"Look Bri." He pointed toward the mountain in the distance. "Do you see that?"

She followed his arm, looking out into the darkness, but what she saw made no sense. A bright round light was dancing in the distance, no not dancing, hovering right above the ground. The purity of the light blinded her as it darted across the sand. Each time she blinked, she could still see its pattern displayed on the back of her eyelids.

"What is it?" she whispered.

"I don't know," Brad replied. "But I don't think we should sit here and wait to find out."

The wind gusted around them making a cyclone out of her long hair. Brianna looked over her shoulder at the fury of the electrical storm. "We can't leave the Bug here. We just finished fixing up the interior."

Brad hadn't taken his eyes off the strange lights in the distance. "We can't stay here, Bri. We've gotta find a place to wait this out." He opened the door and slid out of his seat. "Come on. No sudden movements."

"This isn't the X-Files. I'm sure there's an

explanation."

Before she could say another word, the light sped across the desert straight toward them.

"Get down!" Brad screamed.

Brianna hit the pavement with a squeal as the light passed over them. Brad was scooting under the car, his hand outstretched toward her. "Come on, Bri! Grab my hand."

The pavement was still hot, burning right through her shorts and tank top. Sliding on her stomach, she reached for his hand. Brad clutched her wrist and pulled her under the car beside him. Wrapping his arm around her, he tugged her even closer, shielding her as best he could. Tiny glass shards and rocks scraped into the soft skin of her palms and knees. Sweat dripped off of her nose as she baked between the Bug's hot engine and the heat of the desert highway.

Blinding light surrounded the car, and then moved around the edges slowly. Her heart fluttered in her chest.

"It's looking for us," she whimpered.

"We don't know what it's doing," Brad whispered.

Thunder crashed again. Without any preamble of sprinkling, the sky opened up and heavy rain pelted the pavement. The Bug groaned over them as the wind tore at the bumper. The bright light shifted toward the front of the car, moving closer to the ground.

"Don't look at it!" Brad yelled as the rain turned into a thunderous hail.

But she couldn't look away. The light was hypnotic. She'd never seen anything like it before. Unable to stop herself, Brianna brought her hand up, reaching out toward the ball of light. Brad was yelling something, but she couldn't hear him over the roar of the storm. Brianna wriggled, stretching, trying to free herself from his grip as the light beckoned her.

Electricity suddenly shot through the darkness, exploding in front of her, spearing the pavement. A high pitched screech cut through the storm, exploding the windshield above them. Brad yanked her back. She covered her face as the glass rained down.

The spell was broken.

They stayed hidden under the car until the storm finally moved past them. "Are you ok?" he whispered.

"I think so. Is it gone?"

"I don't see anything. Maybe it followed the storm."

He started to move, but she caught his arm. "No, don't. We should just wait. Someone will drive by eventually."

"Will they?" he asked. "We haven't seen a car all night."

A chill shot down her spine as the revelation struck her. "You're right. That's... Not possible. This is the only highway to Los Angeles."

"It's usually busy, but not tonight. Maybe they put out a storm watch or something. The highway patrol might've closed the freeway."

She knew he was grasping at straws now. Anything to explain what was happening to them. But a rational explanation for what they'd witnessed seemed impossible.

They remained under the car until her legs were cramping. No amount of shifting seemed to help. Still no other vehicles passed by.

Brad grunted, turning on his side to face her. "I can't stay under here any longer. I'm going to get out and have a look around. Okay?"

"Not without me, you're not." She shook her head. "If you're going, then I'm going with you."

He nodded and started to drag himself across the pavement until he could roll away from the VW. Brianna scooted out from the other side and groaned as she pushed herself up. Moonlight shone on the wet highway. The air felt thick and heavy. Puddles baked on the asphalt.

She stretched her back, wiping sweat from her brow as she searched for signs of traffic. Brad stood up on the other side of the car surveying the damage.

"I can't believe there aren't any other cars," she said. "The storm blew over. They wouldn't still have the freeway closed."

"Maybe it's just really late." Brad checked his watch and frowned. "My watch stopped."

Brianna checked hers. "Mine too. That's weird."

Brad nodded and started making his way around the front of the car. "Jesus!"

"What's wro–" Brianna's voice trailed off when she saw what rested at Brad's feet.

A round disc was embedded in the pavement. Smoke rose up from the charred carcass of twisted metal. "Is that a UFO?"

Brad shrugged, his brow furrowed. "I don't know, but whatever it is... It's bleeding."

"What?" She bent down for a closer view. Thick liquid seeped through the seams of the disc. "Maybe it's oil or something."

"Maybe."

But he didn't sound convinced. Before she could say anything, red and blue lights flashed in the distance.

"It's about time," he said.

The black unmarked sedan stopped behind her VW Bug convertible. A tall, thin man dressed in a dark gray pinstriped suit exited the vehicle. His partner climbed out of the passenger side in a coffee brown suit with a red pocket square.

They both wore dark glasses which struck Brianna as odd since it was the middle of the night. Without a word, the driver approached front of her car and stared down at the twisted metal.

"It's over here," he called to his partner.

The man in the brown suit walked over and withdrew a slim digital camera from the inside of his jacket. After snapping a few photos, he turned toward Brianna and Brad, nodded and then walked back to his car without a word.

Brianna turned to the driver. "That's it? Who are you guys?"

"I'm Agent Smith, and that was Agent Jones. We're from the National Weather Service."

Brad rolled his eyes. "Oh Please!" He pointed to the crushed disc in the highway. "Okay Bri, this is when they tell us some bullshit story. Guess what this is supposed to be? Not an alien or a spaceship, no way! What is it *really* Agent Smith, huh? Is it a weather balloon or wait, maybe swamp gas in the middle of the desert?"

"I'm not at liberty to answer that."

Agent Jones returned with a white tarp and a crowbar and went to work, prying the disc out of the highway. Brianna couldn't believe her eyes. Were they going to put the spaceship in their car and just drive away?

She looked up at Agent Smith. "What're you going to do with it?"

He knelt down to assist Agent Jones in wrapping up the metal disc. When he straightened, he turned to Brianna. "On behalf of the National Weather Service, I apologize for any inconvenience this has caused."

He spun on his heel and went back to his car without even looking back.

"That's it?" Brad yelled. "We know what we saw! That wasn't a bullshit weather satellite! We know what we saw!"

The black sedan peppered them with gravel as it sped away from the shoulder.

Agent Smith watched the humans get smaller in the rearview mirror until they disappeared. He reached behind his neck with one hand and started tearing off the latex that covered his red pitted head.

His long black tongue slid between his razor-sharp teeth to wet his thin, reptilian lips as he tugged off his human gloves. He stretched out his scaled hands, his claws tapping the steering wheel along with the beat of the music on the radio.

Agent Jones already had his false head off, and pulled at the latex covering his hands. He rubbed his gnarled green fingers together.

"I hate these damn human suits. They're hotter than Hell and not in a good way!"

"Next time we skeet shoot in the desert, we've gotta start the storms earlier to clear the humans off the roads. The Master will be pissed if he finds out we were out playing and humans saw us. Think they bought it?"

"What that we were trying to cover up some kind of Close Encounter?" He shrugged. "Course they did! Humans always believe in UFOs, especially when we tell them not to. We blew out their windshield, and I even stopped their watches. They don't suspect a thing."

The demons' maniacal laughter echoed across the barren valley as the sedan slid down an embankment and vanished into the darkness.

"Stupid humans! There are no such things as aliens..."

The End

Invaders

They came from beyond the Milky Way. Tiny little creatures with innocent eyes and evil hearts infiltrated the human world with ease. Everyone expected green skinned, mongoloid-headed invaders with long fingers and inhumanly large black eyes.

But these aliens were crafty.

Harlan Kless wasn't fooled.

It all began a few days ago after he finished feeding his annual pumpkin pie fetish. While he was sitting on his porch waiting for his body to finish digesting the mass of his Thanksgiving feast, he noticed something skitter away out of the corner of his eye. Frowning, he made a slow scan of the area. Dry fall leaves covered the browning grass, foreshadowing the snow that was soon to follow. The only noise was the steady drip from the spigot at the corner of the house.

He waited, holding his breath. Surely the leaves would crackle when the yard varmint moved again. His eyes narrowed, searching every shadow. Patience was one of Harlan's best virtues. He could wait out ketchup without tapping the bottle, and paint drying on the fence.

Whatever was wiggling in his yard, he'd see it. Eventually.

A gust of wind broke the tense silence, scattering the brittle leaves, swirling them up from the ground. And that's when he noticed it.

Most people would have mistaken the alien for a squirrel, but Harlan wasn't fooled. Just as the leaves blew away, he saw the rodent's eyes flash crimson, and instead of the clicks and chirps of a squirrel, he heard whispers on the wind. Harlan jumped up out of his chair and bolted down the stairs after the creature. The damned furball jumped to the top of the eight-foot high fence, and from there to the tree in the neighbor's yard. By the time Harlan reached the fence, the would-be squirrel was long gone.

"Goddamn it!" He bent over, struggling to catch his breath. When the wheezing calmed, he straightened up shaking his head. "I know you're out there. You don't fool me, you little bastard."

He waited for an answer, scanning the trees. The wind swirled, mussing his thinning white hair and sending a chill down his spine, but he didn't move. After half an hour passed, Harlan grumbled and headed back to his house.

That night he turned off his cell phone and wrapped his satellite dish in aluminum foil. He'd miss watching Judge Judy, but there was no way in Hell he was going to sit by and let alien rodents use him for inter-galactic communications. Next he ripped the cords out of the back of his computer severing his last avenue for communication with the outside world.

It was a week before he saw the aliens again.

He'd just finished stashing the last of his groceries, packing the pantry with a few months worth of rations just in case he had to turn his home into a bomb shelter. Every once in a while when the wind blew just right, he could hear them whispering. The language was foreign, but he was pretty sure he understood.

They were infiltrating earth and soon the human race would be an endangered species.

Harlan spent the next week mailing off letters to every news station and television talk show he could find, warning them of the impending invasion. He informed them that the safest method of communication was through the postal service, but he didn't receive any replies.

He sat on the porch clutching his shotgun the day his nephew drove up.

"Uncle Harlan?" His nephew's brow furrowed when he glanced at the shotgun. "What's going on?"

Never taking his eyes off the tress, knowing his adversaries were watching, Harlan tightened his grip on the barrel. "Keeping watch."

"Watch? Over what?"

"They're here, Thomas. No one believes me, but I've seen them. I can hear them whispering."

"Who's whispering?" He pulled open the screen door and winced. "Oh God Uncle Harlan. The house reeks."

Harlan nodded without looking back. "Course it does. Can't have them going through my garbage, so it's inside."

Thomas knelt down in front of his chair. "I think you should come with me, Uncle Harlan. You can stay at my place and we'll get you in to see Dr. Halberns right away."

He frowned, meeting his nephew's gaze. "I don't need a doctor. These aliens know I'm onto them. They're watching me all the time now. They're worried I'll expose their plot. They're crafty little buggers."

"Uncle Harlan, put down the gun and come with me, all right? You've been alone out here too long." He glanced over at the door and shook his head. "You can't stay here. We can skip the doctor, but I can't leave you here."

Harlan sighed and set his shotgun on the table bedside him. "You don't believe me either."

"I got your letter about the squirrels and when your phone was out of service and your cell number was disconnected, I thought I'd better get out here to check on you."

"I know what I saw, Thomas."

He nodded. "I'm not saying you didn't see it, Uncle Harlan. But just because you saw something doesn't make it real. You've been alone for a long time. Your mind can start playing tricks on you."

Harlan stood up, bumping the shotgun off the table. "Leave me alone, Thomas."

Thomas dove for the shotgun and pumped a cartridge into the chamber, aiming the barrel at Harlan's chest. "I can't do that, Uncle."

His nephew hissed, whispering foreign words in rapid succession. The alien rodents clustered on the ground, advancing toward Harlan's house.

"No." He shook his head, backing away. "They got to you."

His nephew's mouth twitched, curling into a sick grin as his eyes flashed crimson. "They've gotten everyone, Uncle. Now it's *you* they want."

"No!" Harlan flinched, jarring himself in his chair. He gasped, swiveling his head from side to side. No sign of his nephew or the squirrels. Sitting on the table beside him was an empty pie tin, not the shotgun he was expecting. Gradually his heart rate slowed and he smiled.

"Too much damned pumpkin pie." He chuckled and picked up the pie tin on his way back into the house. Just a dream. A crazy, too-much-pumpkin-pie dream.

As the door closed behind him, hushed whispers echoed on the evening breeze and crimson eyes glowed in the darkness.

The End

The Aviator

As far back as he could remember, he dreamed of flying, of soaring weightless on the wind. Free.

But this wasn't flying. This was falling.

"Save me!" Wade screeched into the violent gusts of wind. The ground raced toward him in a game of chicken he would never win.

His tangled chute flapped above as he tugged, yanked, and pulled at the red back-up cord. But nothing happened. The wind howled, deafening his ears. Wasn't this the part where your life was supposed to flash before your eyes?

"Things are not always what they seem, boy."

Wade's head snapped toward the voice.

His eyes widened behind his safety goggles. It had to be a hallucination.

He blinked hard, but when he opened them again the old man in a black robe still floated in midair beside him, with a huge pair of what looked like pantyhose filled with balloons, countless bright-colored helium-filled balloons. The legs of the hose were tied under his shoulders.

"This is it. I've lost it." Wade struggled to keep from hyperventilating. He could see highways now, with tiny cars.

It wouldn't be long until he couldn't see anything anymore.

The old man shook his head. "Nothing is lost. The power is within you. Look inside."

"I don't have time for reflection. I'm about to be pummeled into the pavement." Wade gave a few more desperate tugs on his back-up rip cord.

"If that is so, then you have nothing to lose. Close your eyes and picture what you need most. Make it real, boy."

The air warmed around him; he could almost make out landmarks below. Whimpering, Wade closed his eyes and instantly pictured wings. His entire body tingled.

Maybe now his life would flash before him. Maybe he'd messed it up because he didn't have his eyes closed. He waited, but no mental film starring him started. Instead, he noticed the wind stopped howling. In fact, it didn't even feel like he was falling anymore.

He cracked one eye open for a tentative look at his predicament. Both eyes popped open when he realized gravity was no longer his executioner. In fact, he shifted, turning with the wind.

He was flying.

Laughter bubbled up from his throat, but exited his mouth as the screech of an eagle. Wade frowned and glanced down to see feathers. Panic seized him again and he lost his rhythm with the wind. Flapping wildly, he struggled to keep from falling. He searched for the strange old man with the balloons, but he was nowhere to be seen.

Batting his wings into the wind, he soared almost as quickly as his mind raced. He couldn't possibly be a bird, right? Maybe he was dreaming, although he could remember paying the pilot and the skydiving school that morning.

Money didn't usually change hands in dreams.

He needed to get his feet back on the ground safely first. He could worry about how none of this could possibly be real later.

He stretched out his wingspan, tilting to the right, and circled a large Sequoia tree. With open talons, he grappled for a hold on a branch. His velocity came to a screeching halt, and he fluttered his wings to keep from losing his balance.

Back on earth and he wasn't dead. Amazing.

Before he could examine his predicament any further, the old man hovered in the air beside him again. "Fine work, boy."

He tried to speak, but all that came out were frustrated squawks.

"The same way you found your wings, you will discover your legs again." He glanced down below and then back up at Wade. "Be careful what you wish for up here, boy. It's still a long way down."

Wade tilted his head to see the ground and realized the old man was right. Even if he could change back, doing it up here would kill him. He gave his wings a tentative flap, shifting his feathers and finally shot out from the branch. Instead of falling, he glided through the air.

He shouted, and the eagle's cry echoed through the trees. Gradually he circled lower until he felt his feet touch the earth.

"Nicely done, boy. Now close your eyes and picture yourself as you were."

How did the crazy old man get around so quickly?

Wade closed his eyes and concentrated on seeing himself walking to the plane with his pack on his back. His limbs started to tingle and he held his breath.

"You learn fast."

He opened his eyes and saw the old man, then peered down at his feet and saw… shoes! He grinned. "This is impossible."

The man shook his head with a twinkle in his eyes. "Not for you. You're the aviator."

"The what?"

His hand vanished into his black robe and returned with a large gold ring. He slipped it onto Wade's finger. "This belongs to you."

In the center of the ring was a flat tiger's eye stone and words were inscribed around the edge. "What does it say?"

"It's Latin for the circle of power."

Wade's brow creased in confusion. "Why are you giving this to me?"

"Every generation ushers in a new circle. One protects the land, one the sea, one the air, and one the circle itself. We are chosen before our birth to keep the world safe. You are the Aviator. You can take any form that flies."

Wade's mind buzzed. "Anything?"

The old man's eyes sparkled. "Yes. If you picture it in your mind, your vision will become your body."

"And you're the protector of the circle?"

He shook his head. "No."

"Then why are you helping me?"

A wistful smile curved on his wrinkled face. "Because my time is done. My ring is yours."

"You were the Aviator?"

He nodded. "I was. And now you will be."

"B-but I don't know how to be an aviator," Wade stammered. "Who are the other protectors? If I believed in this, how would I find them?"

"The circle will bring you together." He clasped Wade's shoulder. "Give me one last wish?"

"Last wish?" He frowned. "Are you dying?"

"Fading. From this world to the next." He untied the balloons and set them free, then stared at Wade. "Take me for one last flight."

"What?" Wade twisted the ring on his finger, trying to yank it free, but it wouldn't budge.

"Fate can't be changed, boy." The old man straightened his robe. "Now close your eyes and picture something large and fantastic."

Wade followed directions and closed his eyes. Suddenly a dragon filled his mind. Could he become something make-believe? Could dragons really fly? His body started tingling and he focused on details. He would be a large red dragon with charcoal wings. When he opened his eyes, the old man smiled and stroked his large muzzle.

"You are going to make a fine Aviator."

Wade lowered his wing and the old man crawled up until he was seated atop dragon's broad back. "Let's fly."

The beast shook his head and pumped his powerful wings until he zipped up and burst into the sky above the forest. Flying higher and higher, out toward the sea, the old man's gleeful laughter buoyed his winged steed.

Somewhere over the sea, Wade noticed the old man's laughter faded along with his body. The dragon roared into the wind and mourned as a new weight settled onto his massive shoulders.

I am The Aviator.

The End

In the Dead of Winter

Morozko walked through the pristine forest of white, admiring the fresh canvas of desolate ice that covered the mountain ranges. No creature, human or otherwise, disturbed the silence that wrapped him in its suffocating embrace. The chill fed his wintry soul, and left behind a hint of a smile on his blue lips.

He savored the last spoonful of mint chocolate chip ice cream, careful not to lose a single drop, lest he add color to his kingdom of white. He quietly disposed of the ice cream container in a nearby trash can. Not all of America was bad. He had grown fond of their ice cream over the years, relishing the frigid creamy treat when he could. Spring would be visiting this continent soon, so he would be moving on.

But not today. Today was still his paradise, his time, his winter.

He turned his silver eyes up to the mountain tops and nodded his own approval. This was a fine frost. Even the approaching sunlight, barely peering over the mountain's peaks could not damage his perfect creation.

Since the dawn of time, he had lived by many names, Old Man Winter, Jack Frost, Jokul to the Norsemen, and the Finnish had called him Kalevala. The Americans had even portrayed him as the Coldmiser on a television special, but he preferred Morozko.

He was born into the bleak, biting, bitter winds of Siberia, nursed by her blizzards, and strengthened by her unyielding winter, so it seemed fitting to refer to him by his Russian name, Morozko.

His only love had called him by that name.

The Russian people still pass down his story from generation to generation. They share the tale of an unwanted daughter who was left in the frozen forest, only to meet Morozko.

That much was true.

But unlike the fairy tale, his beautiful Anya never made it back home alive.

His jaw clenched at the memory. The centuries-old wound was forever raw, never fully healed, immortally painful. Perfect.

Silently he made his way up higher, away from the quaint town of Squaw Valley, toward the void of the snow capped peaks. His body left no footprints behind.

He was one with the ice.

Weaving through the towering pine trees, he hiked, marveling at the wintry morning quiet. One sound could break the spell, and at the same time, the ice that tenuously held ton after ton of snow. A single crack could cut through the silence, and send a tidal wave of snow to blanket the village below.

His lips twitched at the thought.

When he finally reached the peak, he stared down at the town. The skiers and the shop owners stirred. Activity spilled out onto the sidewalks, and a faint hum rose up as the ski lifts came to life. His silver eyes narrowed, watching the skiers rise up on gondolas with no concept of what awaited them.

These were his favorite casualties. Great pride goes before the fall...

And fall they would.

He would see to it as he had been doing for centuries.

But it wouldn't bring Anya back.

He clenched his cold fists and waited.

Nothing would bring Anya back, and therefore he would punish the mortals every winter for bringing her into his world, knowing his love would kill her. An icy tear sparkled at the corner of his eye.

She awakened his cold heart so long ago.

He'd found her freezing in the forest, abandoned by her own father. When he asked her if she needed shelter, instead of begging for rescue, his beautiful Anya, saw his true self. She saw Morozko, the father of winter, the bringer of ice and snow, and in spite of her shivering; she offered him a smile and praised him for the beautiful snow.

Something in that moment changed him forever. The sound of her voice didn't shatter his precious silence, it sung over it, colored it without corrupting the vast blanket of white.

And in that instant, he loved her.

But Anya was not of his winter world. She was human, and the sting of the cold had already delivered her lungs a mortal wound he would never be able to heal. He'd wrapped her in furs, but holding her in his arms, only served to chill her body further.

Their love bloomed for several weeks, but it was a short-lived blossom, ending with pneumonia stealing the color from her skin.

"One kiss, my love," she had whispered.

"I cannot." His chest tightened, aching. "My lips are ice, Anya. You need warmth."

"I need you." Another fit of coughing

seized her voice.

    Scarlet drops of her blood desecrated the white snow, as her body fought for air. He held her, knowing he couldn't warm her; and loved her, knowing his love would force him to lose her. She trembled, her shallow breaths echoed with a gurgle of liquid where there should be none.

    His cold heart shattered, rupturing into shards of bitterness, until he thought he might die from the ache of watching her life slip away.

    Her pale hand reached up to caress his chilled face as she whispered, "No regrets, Milaya moya." Coughing stole her voice again. She met his eyes and whispered, "You have my love... Always."

    She drew him closer for one last kiss. "Do novyh vstrech."

    Her eyes closed and he held her until her ragged breathing slowed and finally he felt her sigh as if her soul had escaped up to the heavens, leaving him behind with only a shell of the woman who had brought spring into his winter world.

    "Dos vidaniya, Solnyshko moyo." His grief swelled into a blizzard that wiped out the surrounding villages. He didn't care. The villagers had sent her to him, knowing she did not belong in his world.

    It was their fault she was dead.

    Taking a deep breath, Morozko watched the

extreme skiers climbing up the mountain toward him. They wore their pride and their egos as if they were a rare badge of honor.

But today would be their final run. He would make it so.

His grey eyes narrowed, and his hair blew around him as the snow flurries rose up to surround their father. Slowly he raised his cold hands toward the winter sky.

Today marked the anniversary of Anya's death.

And today the cold-hearted god would again unleash his fury at fate, destiny, and the world of mankind. He tipped his head back and bellowed forth his rage.

The avalanche echoed in reply until the rumble became a thundering roar. He watched with a bitter cold smile, as the tidal wave of white smothered all traces of humankind below him.

The silence returned, deafening and beautiful, and with his anger once more appeased, ancient Morozko turned and walked away without a word.

The End

Do novyh vstrech. – Til we meet again.
Milaya moya. – My love
Dos vidaniya, Solnyshko moyo – Goodbye my Sunlight.

Unemployed Muses Anonymous

Mel fed the parking meter some quarters and hurried down the sidewalk. The large black leather attaché case thumped against her back with each stride. After checking her watch, she kicked up her pace a notch.

When she reached the bookstore, she rounded the corner and punched in her entry code into the number pad. The red door clicked as the lock opened. She yanked open the door and stepped into the shadows.

Today was going to be a big day for UMA. Today was the day they started a new marketing campaign. Zeus could leave them stranded in the mortal world, but he couldn't stop them from working.

Not anymore.

She flipped on the light switch, bathing the empty conference room in florescent light. The long walnut table was flanked by nine high-backed leather executive chairs; soon to be filled by her sisters.

Mel placed the bag at the head of the table and carefully withdrew her weeping mask. With the emblem safely resting beside her place at the table, she pulled out her laptop and the projector. While she tested some power point slides up on the wall of the conference room, her sister, Calliope, came in with her writing pad.

"Hi Mel. This is an exciting day isn't it?"

"I hope it will be." Mel found it difficult to stay positive. It went against her nature as the muse of tragic poetry, but she did her best to overcome it.

Getting dates with a name like Melpomene was tough on its own, but wrap that up with an obsession with tragedy, and she could be a very lonely muse. "Do you have all the business projections for Les Neuf Soeurs?"

"I do." She nodded with a smile. "This is going to be huge! I can't believe we didn't think of it sooner."

Mel smiled. Cal was the muse of epic poetry, so being realistic wasn't really her strong suit. The sky was the limit with Cal.

Down the hall, Mel heard humming. "Sounds like Era and Terp are on their way."

Erato and Euterpe were the muses for music and lyrics. They almost always traveled together, and usually people heard them coming.

"Good morning Cal," Era said in a bright shining voice, adding as she turned, "Oh hello Mel. Do you need any help with the projector?"

"No, it looks like I've got it all figured out. Do you two have the marketing materials ready?"

Terp set down her double-reed aulos beside her place at the table. "Yes, we've got them all ready to go. I even came up with a theme for our commercials."

Picking up her recorder-like flute, Euterpe started to play. Era sang along to part of the melody just as Poly and Psi walked in. Without missing a beat, Polyhymnia joined her sister Era and harmonized the lyrics. Psi smiled and added to the music with her lyre, while jigging around the room.

Mel glanced at the cacophony of art improvising around her and shook her head. This was why none of their plans ever worked out. They were muses for the arts, not for business.

How were they ever going to get anything accomplished with her sisters dancing and singing?

She looked down the table at Cal and sighed. Calliope was busy writing out every detail of her sisters' arrivals, no doubt painting the scene like they were about to embark on an epic quest.

Mel checked her watch. The last three sisters were late. Not that Mel was surprised, but after all these centuries, she thought this time it might be different.

She sighed, envisioning the tragic end to their beautiful idea. It was all she could do to suppress the urge to throw up her hands and cry. Surely it wouldn't turn out as badly in reality as it did in her head.

She hoped.

Laughter interrupted her wallow in the pool of self-pity. Thalia popped through the door along with Clio and Nia. Thalia was the muse for comedy and she lived up to her title. The poor girl remained so playful and prone to uncontrollable laughter that she'd been mistakenly committed to an asylum twice.

Since then, Urania, although she preferred Nia, moved in with her to help keep the mortals away.

Nia was the muse to the stars. Not celebrities, but the stars up in the sky. She always had her compass close by and could find the way home from anywhere.

Clio trudged to her place at the table, ignoring the dancing, singing and laughter that surrounded her. Mel envied her sister. Clio, muse to history, was happiest reliving the past, which made getting her to notice the present challenging at best.

"Hi Clio," Mel said eyeing her sister's scrolls. "You remember why we're meeting today, right?"

Clio nodded. "We're going back to Olympus."

"What?" Mel frowned.

Clio smiled. "Just kidding. Thalia's trying to help me with my sense of humor."

Mel shot a glare at her giggling sister. "Perfect."

She walked around to the head of the table and cleared her throat. "Excuse me. Can we get started?"

The music and laughter gradually died down as the muses placed their emblems onto the tabletop. The walnut conference table glowed with power. Mel smiled and went on. "After selling off some of our relics and vases, we made the down payment on our new building. I hired the architect and Nia will be working with him to design our new theater, Les Neuf Soeurs!"

All the muses applauded, but the phone interrupted their ovation. Mel frowned and lifted the receiver to her ear.

"UMA can I help you?" Mel rolled her eyes. "No. This is Unemployed Muses

Anonymous. She's not here. Really." She paused. "I understand. No problem."

She hung up the phone and looked up to find all eight sisters staring at her. "It was another one of those Uma Thurman calls."

"Oh," was the unison reply.

Mel clicked through the power point, explaining the business plan to her sisters. All of her numbers were very conservative, more due to her nature than any business experience, and her sister muses did their best to fill in their portions.

Cal stood up and presented her epic projections for ticket sales, and Erato and Euterpe sang the new commercial jingle for the radio spot they bought. Of course appluse broke out at the end of their little ditty. Years of unemployment hadn't lessened their skill for music and lyrics.

Then Poly and Psi provided a list of potential theater groups who could use the new facilities. Psi did her best hold still while they presented, but being the muse of dance made it almost impossible for her to keep from wiggling.

Thalia and Nia sat at the other end of the conference table doing their best to focus. If their plans worked out, which Mel had many doubts, then they were the two muses who would be running the office.

Mel watched them, sighing inwardly when she realized they weren't taking any notes. By the end of the power point presentation, Mel wanted to scream, but that wasn't unusual, just another perk of being the tragic muse.

She closed her laptop and looked over at Clio. "Are you ready to bring the history of Les Neuf Soeurs to life for us again?"

She nodded and rose up from her chair with a scroll in hand. Clio was tall and willowy with a porcelain complexion that rivaled the smooth marble of their statues. Brushing her long blond hair behind her shoulders, she took a deep breath.

"Our theater will allow patrons to travel back in time, to Paris in 1776. Les Neuf Soeurs, or in English The Nine Sisters, once helped to inspire free-thinkers like Benjamin Franklin and Thomas Jefferson. These great men encouraged France to help aid in the American Revolution. Without the inspiration we provided, this country might not have existed, and with our help again, this nation will find the inspiration to heal the wounds that ail it. While the government cuts funding for the arts, we will inspire them to look to art for answers. After all, life still imitates art."

She rolled up her scroll and made eye contact with each sister. "We will no longer need UMA. We will no longer be ignored or forgotten. Our gifts will once again be respected, honored and revered."

The conference room erupted in

enthusiastic applause.

Mel raised her hand, quieting her sisters. "I have one more thing to add. A surprise."

"A surprise?" Calliope made a note in the meeting log. "I love surprises."

Mel opened the conference room door and all the muses gasped. A tall chiseled man with olive skin and a mop of dark brown hair stood before them. His features were perfect and his smile would make any mortal woman fall under his spell.

"Good morning, Ladies."

Nia frowned. "Ploutos. What are you doing here? Shouldn't you be polishing Zeus' sandals up on Mt. Olympus?"

He raised a brow. "Melpomene invited me to this meeting. As the god of finance and fortune, she thought I could offer you some support with your business plan."

Nia's jaw dropped. "Mel, you didn't."

"I did," Mel replied. "Can't you see? This is a great idea, but we've had millions of great ideas! It's what we do. We're muses. Look around this table, sisters. Following through on a business proposal is not our strong suit."

Mumbles and grumbles rose up around the conference table as Mel gave Ploutos a nervous shrug. She felt failure's hot breath on the back of her neck, but did her best to hold it off. He kept his shoulders squared, and his posture calm and confident as he sent her an encouraging smile and a wink.

Finally Clio stood. "I'm not thrilled about accepting help from the snobs on Olympus either, but judging by our past endeavors, his business expertise could make all the difference."

Mel couldn't believe her eyes as her sisters started to nod. "So, are we all in agreement? We'll let Ploutos help us make Les Neuf Soeurs a reality?"

After the unanimous vote, the muses collected their emblems and said their goodbyes. Mel stayed behind, packing up her laptop and the projector. Once everyone was gone, she smiled up at Ploutos.

"Thank you for helping us."

He took her hand and pulled her into his arms. "You don't have to thank me. It's a great idea you all came up with. Insane given the state of the economy right now, but it just might work."

She grinned and leaned up to kiss him. He hummed softly against her lips and pulled back with a smile. "You still didn't tell them we're dating."

Mel shook her head. "Baby steps."

"Think they'll ever like me?"

"Probably not." He raised a brow and she smiled. "Coming from *me*, that's a definite maybe so."

He laughed and picked up the laptop and projector. "I never imagined the muse of tragedy would make me so happy."

"Not so crazy. Money and tragedy often walk hand in hand, right?"

"Touché."

Mel turned off the lights and locked the door to UMA headquarters. Ploutos took her hand as they walked back to her car. She couldn't hold back her smile.

For the first time in centuries, it felt good to be a muse again.

The End

Last Dance

I always meant to come back here.

As years crept by, I never forgot that dance. It was a planned mixer for the young officers at Camp Robinson to meet and socialize with the local sorority in North Little Rock, Arkansas.

Now I hardly recognize it.

In my day, we lived in wooden single-story barracks that were more like tiny cottages, all lined up in perfect rows. World War II was in full swing back then, and I had enlisted in the military with all of my buddies from school. I enjoyed my days there. The training was rough, but the camaraderie felt like family. Serving the country I loved and believed made me proud. Fresh out of high school, and I already felt like a man.

Times were simpler back then. I know it's an old man's folly to say that, but it's the God's honest truth. We weren't faced with so many options back then. We were expected to get out of school, get married, and work to support our families.

Simple.

So when I attended the Sweetheart's Dance in 1944, I wasn't looking for a fling. I was looking for forever.

But that was a long time ago.

I lowered myself onto a shady bench, leaning heavily on my cane. Hard to believe I once danced the jitterbug with such gusto. Time is a bitch. She steals away your youth before you notice it's missing, and once it's gone you can't ever get it back.

I met my girl here on Valentine's Day in 1944. The mess hall where the dance took place is long gone, replaced by a new prefabricated metal building. At least they put a plaque out front to remember the intrepid old mess hall building that fed over 25,000 young American men while we trained in the art of war.

When I close my eyes, I can see the landscape as it was, clear crisp colors without the haze of cataracts clouding my view. She was wearing a yellow dress with a yellow rose clipped in her hair.

My old mouth still curls up into a smile at the thought of her. My first true love.

Our eyes met across the smoke filled room and my heart skipped a beat. My God she was an angel. I mustered my courage, puffed out my chest, and walked over to take her hand.

"Good evening, Miss. I'm Private Walker."

Her hand felt so perfect inside of mine. Her cheeks flushed with color, and I was sure I'd never seen anything so beautiful in all my life.

"Pleased to meet you, Private Walker. I'm Betty Joe Crawford."

"Could I have this dance, Betty Joe?"

She nodded and we stepped onto the dance floor.

A cool breeze brushed over me on the bench, and with my eyes still closed, I was certain I could smell the rose in her hair and the faint scent of her Shalimar perfume. In my mind, I could hear the band and I saw Betty Joe's eyes light up when they started Boogie Woogie Bugle Boy.

Man, that girl could cut a rug.

We danced the night away. Laughing as we hopped around to Shoo Shoo Baby, and gasping when we finished the jitterbug. What a night! We ended the perfect evening slow dancing, cheek to cheek, to Bing Crosby's latest hit, I'll Be Seeing You.

I wasn't ready for the night to end.

"Can I see you again, Betty Joe?"

Her cheeks flushed again as she looked up at me. "I don't even know your first name, Private Walker."

"Billy. Billy Walker. I'm from California."

Her smile made my knees wobble, and her dark brown eyes sparkled up at me. "I would love to see you again, William Walker."

That was the first time anyone had ever called me William.

I wanted to kiss her in the worst way, but there were chaperones ushering everyone out, and I didn't want to embarrass Betty Joe. Instead we planned to meet at the malt shop the very next evening.

We had a date every night for the next six weeks before I transferred overseas. I ended up in the Battle of Cassino in Italy. As part of the artillery, we shelled the Nazis for days through heavy thunderstorms. A few of my friends ended up with pneumonia. Gary Shore never recovered.

On the bench, I coughed, my ancient lungs rasped and burned, but I didn't open my eyes. I wasn't ready to leave the past just yet. The ache in my chest smoldered, but I pushed it away and focused on my days in Italy in 1944.

Better days.

I wrote to Betty Joe every night. I told her about the battle, and later I wrote to her about watching Mt. Vesuvius erupt. I'd never seen anything like it. I wrote a letter about the rain and the snow, even shared my review of Irving Berlin's new show "This is the Army." He brought it all the way over to Italy for us. Most importantly I wrote about how much I missed her, and loved her. I couldn't wait to get back home.

But one day I received a letter that wasn't in her handwriting.

No, I didn't want to remember this part. I struggled to open my eyes, but I couldn't. My heart fluttered. I couldn't catch my breath. I coughed, and for a moment I saw the metal building, but my eyes drifted closed again.

Lost in my memories, I was opening the letter from Mr. and Mrs. Crawford. Their dearest Betty Joe was dying of tuberculosis. She asked them to write this letter to let me know I would always have her undying love.

Back on the bench, I felt a hot tear spill down my cheek, but I was too weak to lift my hand to wipe it away.

"William? William, is that you?"

It was so dark. I couldn't see a thing, but I knew that voice. I hadn't heard it in over sixty years, but without a doubt, I knew it was Betty Joe. I tried to answer her, but my body wouldn't respond. I couldn't make a sound. My lungs burned.

Part of me panicked, while another part of me welcomed the inevitable. In the distance a familiar melody caressed my ears. Our song. One last breath heaved from my tired lungs, and then my eyes fluttered open and I could see again. No haze of cataracts, no glasses, and there, not a hundred feet from me, was Betty Joe. She smiled at me in her yellow dress with a rose in her hair, and somewhere Bing was singing our song.

I glanced back over my shoulder and saw a time worn old body I hardly recognized, slumped over on the bench with a bittersweet smile on his lips and a tear still shining on his cheek.

"William?"

Turning back toward her voice, I realized the arthritis that had pained my knees for the past twenty years was gone. I was free.

"I've missed you, William."

"I'm sorry it took me so long to get back."

She smiled and touched my cheek. "You were always worth waiting for."

I took Betty Joe into my arms and kissed her while Bing crooned:

> *I'll be seeing you in every lovely summer's day,*
> *In everything that's light and gay,*
> *I'll always think of you that way.*

I'll find you in the mornin' sun
And when the night is new
I'll be looking at the moon
But I'll be seeing you...

I was finally home.

The End

Stranded

I'm writing this story down so that I won't forget the details later. I'm writing it so I'll know that it wasn't a dream. I'm writing this story because I'm too damned scared to say the words out loud.

The sun is shining bright this morning, but my hands are still shaking. I haven't slept in over twenty-four hours. I don't see myself sleeping anytime soon. I guess I should start at the beginning. I used to be a high school English teacher, but now I own Guy's Will Tow You towing service. I'm Guy. I'm the only driver of my only tow truck, a one-man show. My specialty is back country towing. I operate out of Campo, California, about an hour east of San Diego. I know all the back roads and unmarked trails, and when I always have a cooler of bottled water on ice for my thirsty customers.

    I pride myself on service, and survive by a word-of-mouth reputation.

    But this isn't about my business.

    Last night I got a call from a woman in distress. I logged the call at 9pm.

    "Guy here..."

    "Is this the towing service?"

    I could hardly hear her, but cell phone service is usually tough out in these parts. I cranked up the volume on my cordless phone.

    "Yeah it is... Can I help you?"

    "I'm stranded with my two children."

    "No problem. Where are you?"

    "I'm on the Yuha Cutoff. We were on our way to Coyote Wells."

    "All right, Yuha Cutoff at Imperial Highway?"

    "No," she said. "We're stranded on the Yuha cutoff a few miles from Interstate 8."

    I frowned. "You serious about that?"

    "Of course! Please hurry..."

    Her cell phone signal faded, and I sat there staring at my log book. Scratching my head, I reached for the truck keys. Why would she have taken the cutoff from Interstate 8? That was a desolate route. The Imperial Highway was a new, more direct route. No one used the cutoff anymore. Weird. I put my plate of reheated Chinese food back in the fridge. I could finish up my dinner later. Not like anyone was eating with me anyway.

I finished logging the trouble call in my notebook, grabbed what was left of the sleeve of Girl Scout Trefoil cookies, and headed for the truck. Yeah, we have Girl Scouts all the way out in Campo. Go figure. And even though I only buy the shortbread trefoil cookies, the girls still deliver them out to my place every year and thank me for my support.

I missed my Girl Scout. Maybe she wouldn't be a girl scout anymore. Tracy would be in high school by now. God had she really died that long ago? It hurt like it just happened yesterday.

Shoving the memories aside, I popped a cookie in my mouth and fired up the engine. I could be at the Yuha cutoff in a half hour.

Hot wind gusted through the windows of my cab, while my Creedence Clearwater Revival CD bellowed out the speakers. There wasn't clear radio reception out this way, so CCR kept me company on the solitary trek. It was too quiet on the highway at night; too easy to get lost in my thoughts. Instead I ate another cookie and cranked up the stereo.

Interstate 8 going east into the desert during the week was a pretty deserted highway. No weekend warriors in their campers towing trailers full of dirt bikes shared the road with me, only an occasional semi-truck heading west toward San Diego with deliveries.

When I pulled off the interstate onto the Yuha cutoff, I slowed, scanning the shoulder for any sign of a vehicle. There aren't any street lights in this part of the desert, so I had to depend on my truck's headlights.

Even with my high beams on, the darkness prevailed. It was suffocating, surrounding my rig in a thick blanket of pitch black night. It was easy to believe you were the only person left on earth.

I tapped my fingers against the steering wheel, singing along with CCR.

"*I hear hurricanes a blowin'*
I know the end is comin' soon
I feel the rivers overflowin'
I hear the voice of rage and ruin!"

Out of the blackness on my right a coyote loped into the road.

"Holy Shit!" I jerked the wheel hard to the left. The back of my truck fish-tailed. I turned into the skid and finally righted myself before sliding back over into the right lane again.

    Sweat beaded on my forehead, and I had to swallow my heart back into my chest. A person could wreck out this way and the vultures would find your body before any rescuers did.

    "There's a bad moon on the rise... All right..." CCR sang.

    I took a deep breath and kept looking for a stranded car. I didn't get the license number or make and model before her cell phone dumped out, but I figured there would only be one on this stretch of empty road. If I could find it. The only moon out tonight was in the song on my radio.

    "Hope you got your things together

    Hope you are quite prepared to die.

    Looks like we're in for nasty weather.

    What now you're thinkin' for an eye."

    I was pretty sure that last line was wrong, but hell if I knew what John Fogerty was really saying.

    Finally I saw a woman standing on the right shoulder waving her arms. This had to be my caller. I hit the emergency lights on the truck, and slowed to pull off onto the sandy shoulder. Sliding out from behind the wheel, I slammed the door and the lady rushed over to meet me.

    The wind whipped her hair across her face. From what I could see in the truck lights, she looked like she'd been crying. I glanced ahead, but there wasn't any sign of a car.

"Thank God you're here. You've gotta help us."

I stared down at her and nodded. "Will do. Where's your car?"

She turned and pointed south into the desert. My yellow emergency lights spun around the top of my truck, but I still couldn't see any sign of a car in the brief moments of illumination.

"Out there? How'd you get way out there?"

"I don't know. Please help me. My kids are still in the car. I can't get them out."

My inner alarm bells started going off. Why was her car so far off the road? And why would she leave her kids alone in the dark?

If this had been a man, I probably would've gotten back in my truck and radioed the highway patrol, but this woman was all of five foot two, and I was pretty sure I could defend myself, not to mention that the panic in her eyes looked real. I'd seen enough folks after car accidents to recognize that numb look of shock.

"Let me get my flashlight."

Tears flooded her eyes. "Thank you..."

I nodded and once I had my flashlight we headed south from the road. Walking through the scrub brush and sand, I kept looking for tire tracks, any sign of how she ended up out here, but so far there was nothing. Maybe the wind had already erased them, that's what I told myself anyway.

In the distance, I saw a car. As we got closer, I could see it was a nineties model Toyota Tercel, but the tires were sun-rotted and flat. Sand rested along the windshield wipers, and both the driver's side and passenger side windows were smashed.

A chill shot down my spine. "What's going on here?"

"I already told you," she said. "We're stranded."

"Lady, this car has been here for a long time. I don't know what you're trying to pull..."

She shook her head, and for a split second, it looked like the wind was going to blow her over. "Please help me. I can't leave them in the car." Her dark eyes stared up at me like she could see directly into my soul. "Please Guy. Help us."

I puffed out a sigh, and my common sense along with it, and headed toward the old Tercel. I wasn't prepared for what I found.

The beam from my flashlight cast shadows inside the car, surprising a desert scorpion. The scavenger disappeared into the darkness as I got closer to the Toyota. I bent down to look into the back seat, reassuring the kids.

"Hey back there. I'm here to help you and your Mom..."

My words died away in the wind. In the backseat of the car, under a thick blanket of dirt and sand, sat two small skeletons still dressed in footed pajamas that were now faded by the harsh desert sun. Each tiny torso had a matching blackened hole through their chests. Their hands were still clasped together, resting on the seat between them.

My stomach started retching as I stumbled back from the weather-beaten car. I wiped what was left of my dinner off my chin and spun around to look at her.

"What the Hell??? What is this?"

She wiped the tears from her cheeks. "I couldn't leave them here. Not like this."

"But they're..."

"They're dead," she said very quietly. "I've been trying to get help, but no one comes out this way."

"I don't understand." I felt a bead of cold sweat trickle down my back. "Why didn't you call the highway patrol. Did you just find them today? Why me?"

"You'll call the authorities, right? Make sure they find us."

"Us? What the Hell are you talking about?"

"He killed me first. Over there." She pointed behind the car.

"So you're..."

But she was gone. I swung my flashlight around me, searching for any sign of her. My heart raced, and I ran past the car in the direction she pointed until I almost tripped over what was left of a human skeleton. The shredded terrycloth remnants resembled the outfit of the woman who flagged me down, but I still couldn't believe it until I saw the shoes. The bleached bones in the sand were wearing a pair of faded Reebok tennis shoes. The same style as the woman who led me out there.

I stumbled backwards shaking my head. "This can't be. Can't be..."

"Please say you'll help us." She appeared again beside me. "We've been lost out here for so long."

I shrieked. Just like a little girl. I'm only human, and now I knew that this woman standing right in front of me wasn't. Not anymore.

"Who did this? How is this possible? How did you call me? I..." I couldn't form another clear sentence. My mind was bound up somewhere between the body on the ground and the woman speaking to me.

"Tracy told me to call you."

My heart stopped and I looked over at her. I tried to speak, but all that came out was a raspy whisper, "How do you know..."

"She's a sweet girl. She watches over you

and her Mom. She told me you had a tow truck. She said you would help us."

A gust of hot wind pummeled my face and I realized my cheeks were wet. How long had I been crying?

"Is she out here too?"

She shook her head. "No, not right now."

"I used to be a teacher." Why was I telling her this? "I quit after I lost Tracy. I quit everything. My marriage, my job, my life..." My eyes met the woman's, and even though I knew she wasn't alive, I could still see the pain. She knew my pain. "I miss her so much."

She reached for my hand, but instead of feeling her touch, my skin tingled. I shivered at the cool chill. "She misses you... and Gina."

Gina. My wife. The woman I couldn't comfort. The woman I abandoned when I made grief my mistress.

Pain gripped my chest and twisted. My wounds were opened wide. I knew if I surrendered to the threatening sobs, I may never stop crying. If Tracy thought I would help this woman and her children then that was exactly what I was going to do. I didn't understand any of it, but I did know I would do anything for my little girl.

I wiped my eyes, my nose, and fought for some semblance of self-control. "Ok... Ok. Tell me what can I do. How can I help you?"

"Just call the authorities and tell them where we are. My family has been searching for us, but no one knows he stole a car and brought us out here. We don't want to be stranded in the desert forever. We just want to go home."

I nodded. "I can do that. I've got a CB in the truck. I'll radio for someone. Can you do something for me?"

"I can try," she said.

"Tell Tracy I love her."

"She already knows. She worries about you and her Mom," she said. "Take care, Guy. And thank you..."

And she was gone again.

This time I didn't swing my flashlight around in search of her. I didn't try to understand what was happening. I just walked back to my truck and radioed the highway patrol.

***

So it's been a long night, but I'm finally back home. My hands are still shaking as I finish writing this. I pulled my Chinese food back out of the fridge, I even warmed it up again, but I'm not hungry. Instead I crack open the fortune cookie and I have to chuckle at the slip of paper inside:

Ghosts of the past will shape your future
That's an understatement.

I drop the fortune on the table and head over to my desk. Taking a deep breath, I tug open the top right drawer and pull out a small framed picture of the two people I cherish most in this world. Gina and Tracy smile back at me.

For the first time since I lost my little girl, it's not pain I feel, but love. I run my thumb along her precious cheek and for a moment I can almost hear her laughter again. Maybe I'm delirious from sleep deprivation, but if this night has taught me anything, it's not to question "why" so much.

I set the frame up on my desk and reach back into the drawer for my little phone book. With one last look at Gina's smile, I dial the number and hold my breath.

"Gina? Yeah, it's me..."

The End

The Mission

His mission started with a forgotten Valentine.

Gary found the tattered old card at the bottom of a box of military mementoes his daughter had dropped by the retirement home. Home was a very subjective word, more like a jail for old folks whose kids didn't want to deal with them anymore.

He sighed and waved back to his daughter Sarah as she drove away. Ok, maybe all the kids weren't to blame, but either way, since he broke his hip he needed more help than his only daughter could give. She had three of her own all under ten years old. He didn't really want to be her fourth, very wrinkly and way over ten year old kid.

Nah, it was better this way. They could keep pretending that he was getting better and that eventually he'd be out of the nursing home and back on his own again. At least Sarah hadn't sold his house yet. She did find a renter, but technically he could still move back home. Someday.

But today he had other plans.

He carefully lifted the back flap of the envelope. The yellowed paper cracked and groaned, but it didn't tear. His fingers trembled as he drew out the card. The front had a faded red heart with a Zeppelin that read *I'm up in the air over you!* A smile crept across his ashen face. It seemed like lifetimes ago since the big zeppelins were making transatlantic flights from New York to Europe, but holding this tiny card in his hand brought it all back.

Memories that might be better left in the past.

He looked around the lobby, and once he was certain none of the other residents were around to pepper him with questions, Gary slowly lifted the front of the card to reveal the ornate handwritten script inside. His heart clenched in his chest when he saw her name at the bottom.

All My Heart Always,
Abigail

Lifting it to his face, he sighed. The scent of her perfume was long gone, but remained vivid in his mind. She always smelled like roses, and all of the notes he received while he was in Korea with the Air Force carried her scent.

He thought he had gotten rid of all her letters decades ago, but apparently he missed this one. This one forgotten Valentine.

Why now?

He closed the card and tucked it back into the envelope, staring at the return address. Why didn't he go to her when he got home? Surely she would have still loved him. She pledged all her heart to him always in every letter.

But that was before he was injured. Before shrapnel peppered his face and took off part of his right ear. Rather than face her rejection, he spared himself more wounds and broke up with her.

Only he never actually told her anything. He just stopped answering her letters.

He shook his head and started toward the dining room with the Valentine safely stashed in the pocket of his brown polyester trousers. The walk down the long hallways leading to the large community room used to fill him with dread. He could still hear his walker scraping against the tile floor, after his hip replacement, announcing his approach a good ten minutes before he arrived.

He had a cane now, but he was still pretty

slow.

Heaving a sigh, Gary picked up the pace, fighting to keep his loafers from shuffling. He made his way into the dining room and wrinkled his nose when the smell hit him.

Fish.

Ugh he hated fish!

"Gary!"

Old Bill Plugman was waving an arthritic hand at him. Gary nodded and hobbled over to their usual table.

"We're having fish," Bill bellowed. Gary had told him a hundred times that he could hear just fine, but Bill saw what was left of Gary's mangled right ear and he screamed at him anyway.

Gary finally gave up trying to shush him.

"I could smell it in the hallway." Gary sat down, grimacing more from the scent of fish than his creaking hip. "What kind is it?"

Bill shouted, "I think it's trout, but I guess it could be bass."

Marion tottered by and muttered, "It's catfish ya ol' coot!"

Gary shook his head. "Whatever damn fish it is, I'm not eatin' it. I'll fill up on vegetables and Jell-o"

All the chatter died away once the food was served. Plenty of soup slurping and clanking of silverware filled the silence, but Gary didn't hear any of it. He was lost in the dusty corners of his memory.

Abigail's voice filled his mind. He could hear her smile in her voice. And she always had a smile for him. They met at the corner market after boot camp. He'd come home for two weeks of leave before he shipped out to flight school. The last thing he had expected was to find the other half of his heart. But there it was, right there in Abigail's smile.

"Didja find everything you needed?" She chimed as she punched buttons on the cash register.

"Yep I sure–" Then their eyes met and he was lost. "Did."

He watched her slender neck as she swallowed and her cheeks flushed with color.

"Good," she said. They stood there, frozen in that moment that seemed to last forever before she giggled and looked at the register. "That'll be two-fifty."

Gary handed her correct change, her fingertips brushing his, and the electricity from that touch surged through his veins.

"What time are you off tonight?"

"Five thirty."

"Can I meet you here and buy you a soda or a malt or something?"

She nodded, and Gary was fairly certain he floated out of that store that day. He and Abigail ended up spending every free moment together. They talked, danced, laughed and even kissed. She cried the day he had to leave. Gary had bought her a tiny rose pin and carefully attached it to her sweater.

"I'll come back for you Abigail."

"You better." A tear rolled down her cheek. "You be careful, Gary."

He drew her into his arms and whispered, "I will Abby. I promise. I love you."

He drove away, watching her grow smaller and smaller in the rearview mirror, and he clenched his jaw, grinding his teeth to hold back tears.

"Gary!"

Bill's screaming yanked him back into the present. He frowned, "What is it, Bill?"

"I been talking to you, an' you been vacant old man. I thought you was losin' it. I almost called the nurse."

Gary shook his head. "Nah, I'm okay. Just been thinkin'." He pushed his plate back and gripped the edge of the table. "I'm finished here. I'll see you later Bill."

He heaved his body up until he was standing upright, or as upright as he got these days. Bill was still yelling something to him, but he wasn't paying any attention. He needed to be alone.

He needed to look at that Valentine again.

Safely away from the dinner melee, he sat on the bench in the entryway and pulled the envelope out of his pocket. He stared at the return address as a plan formed in his mind.

An insane plan.

She couldn't possibly still live there. She might not even still be alive.

His heart clenched a little at the thought. He'd rather not know if Abby was gone from this world. He started to tuck the card away again, but stopped himself.

Could he let her slip through his fingers for a second time?

This card turned up now for a reason. This wasn't some crazy coincidence. It couldn't be.

He set his jaw and gave himself a nod. He was going. Gary got up again and lumbered toward the welcome desk.

"Good Evening Mr. Woods, can I help you?"

"Yes, please call me a taxi."

The large nurse behind the desk lifted a brow and looked up at him over her glasses. "Where do you need to go at this time of night, Mr. Woods?"

Gary could feel his blood pressure rising. He was committed to this mission now, and no big nurse was going to get in his way. He may be over eighty years old, but he was still a man, not a child.

He stared right into her eyes. "That's not really any of your business. Last time I checked, I didn't need your permission to go someplace."

She stood up. "No need to get upset, Mr. Woods. It's my job to be sure you're well taken care of. How can I do that if I don't know where you're going?"

He rolled his eyes, "I'm goin' to see a friend. Now please call me a cab or give me a phone and I'll call myself."

"Let me clear this with the Director. I'll be right back."

Gary watched her waddle down the hall, and then hobbled to the front doors. He'd find a cab himself. The automatic doors slid open and Gary was free. He liked the sound of his cane on the sidewalk. It clicked against the concrete, and his shoes didn't squeak. He wasn't in a nursing home. He was on his own.

On a mission.

But he'd never make it on foot. As he started to pass the park and ride lot, a carpool van parked and the driver hopped out. Gary looked over at him and, with nothing to lose, he called out, "Can you take me across town?"

The young man turned around and smiled, "Only if you're on my carpool route. Sorry about that."

Gary nodded, leaning on his cane to rest his

hip. "That's fine. Can you help me find a cab? If I try to walk across town, I'll be ninety before I get there."

The young man chuckled and checked his watch as he headed over toward Gary. "I guess I'm a little early, I could probably make one more run. Where are you headed?"

"Ash Street."

"Ash? How'd you get all the way over here?

"Oh I live over there at Shady Oaks, but I'm going to see a friend on Ash."

The kid looked past him over at the home before meeting Gary's eyes again. "They know you're going?"

Gary shrugged with a crooked smile. "More or less."

"Does this friend know you're coming?"

"I promised her I would, fifty-eight years ago. I figure I've made her wait long enough."

"Good luck with that Old Man." The kid smiled. "She's gonna be pissed."

"I reckon she might be." Gary nodded and made his way over to the van. Twenty minutes later he was on her street again for the first time in over fifty years.

"You want me to wait for you?"

"Nah," Gary replied, pulling out his worn leather wallet.

"No charge for the ride."

"You sure?"

The kid nodded, "Yeah, this one's on the house. Good luck..."

Gary nodded, sliding his wallet back into his pocket. "Thanks. I probably need it."

The van pulled away and Gary wheezed in a deep breath. Come what may, this was a mission he needed to complete. Abby deserved no less. Even if he couldn't find her or anyone who knew her, he would at least know he tried.

He struggled up the two steps to her porch, or the porch that used to be hers, and stepped forward to the front door. The house was gray now, instead of the yellow he remembered, but other than that, it looked relatively unchanged. He stared at the doorbell for a moment and finally summoned up the courage to press the button. He held his breath and waited.

Just when he thought no one was home, the door creaked open.

"Can I help you?"

It took him a moment to remember why he rang the bell. He stared at the young woman at the door before he found his voice again.

"Abigail Brown? I'm looking for Abigail Brown."

Her brow furrowed and his heart sank.

"Brown?" She shook her head. "My

Grandma is Abby Sinclair."

"Sinclair? Is she here?"

"Who's that at the door Savannah?" A woman called from the other room.

Gary's eyes welled with tears. He knew that voice.

"Tell her it's Gary." He could hear his old ticker pounding in his ears and added, "Tell her sorry it took so long."

The girl looked at him like he was insane and closed the door. He could hear her footsteps as she walked away, and he leaned on his cane, waiting. Would she see him or would she send him away?

God, just hearing her voice again tore him up.

He'd loved his wife. They'd been together for nearly forty years before she passed away, but he had never been swept away by just the sound of her voice. She was a wonderful woman, and their love was a solid foundation in his life, but it had never been all-consuming or passionate.

Until now, hearing Abby's voice again, he'd never recognized the distinction. She awakened the part of his soul that existed only for her.

When the door opened again, the young woman stepped out onto the porch with him. She stared at him for a moment and then took his hand in both of hers.

"I don't know who you are, but Grandma Abigail seems to. She wants me to bring you out back. She's on her favorite porch swing."

His heart skipped a beat, which would normally worry him, but now, he hardly noticed. Gary nodded and let the young woman help him inside.

"Grandma's nearly blind now, so after Grandpa passed away I moved in to help her."

"Your Grandma is an amazing lady."

She nodded and gave him a stern look as she walked him through the house. "You bet she is. You be good to her, Mister."

He gave her hand a squeeze and stepped through the back door.

There was Abby. Her silver hair swept up into a bun, with wisps of loose hair falling down to frame her face. She turned at the sound and smiled.

He could hardly breathe. Pinned to the collar of her blouse was the rose he gave her decades ago.

"It's about time, Gary."

"I'm sorry I'm late."

He made his way to the porch swing and carefully sat down beside her. She brought a hand up to his face, tracing the edge of his jaw, before she slapped him.

Gary gasped.

"You broke my heart, Gary."

"I'm so sorry Abby. I couldn't come back."

"Why?"

He lifted her hand up to his right side, tracing his scars and finally up to his right ear, or what was left of it.

A tear rolled down her cheek. "I wouldn't have cared."

"I was a coward, Abby. I wanted you to remember me like I was."

"I loved who was in here." She pressed her hand to his chest. "I didn't care about the package you came in."

He nodded, clearing the emotion blocking his throat. "I'm so sorry I hurt you Abby. You were the last person in the world I wanted to hurt. I thought you could do much better than a deformed soldier."

"Bah." She waved her hand in the air. "Why are you here, Gary?"

He took the forgotten Valentine out of his pocket and placed it in her hand.

"Because I found this card, and I figured it was time to see if I could find the girl who promised me her heart."

She smiled again, and in spite of the wrinkles, she looked like an angel. "My heart has always been yours."

She slid her hand inside his and their fingers entwined like they'd never parted.

He placed his other hand over hers and whispered, "I've missed you Abby."

And for the first time in over fifty years, Gary and Abby kissed.

"Welcome home," she whispered.

Gary embraced her and closed his eyes. His life was finally complete.

Mission accomplished.

The End

A Pirate's Treasure

Moonlight cast long shadows along the old tree-lined streets as the pirate stalked through the dark tunnel. He didn't need a light. He'd been making this journey for over a century. His leather soled boots scraped against the rugged stone steps. Right, left, right, left, he trudged up from the dark rum cellar.

Rum. Dear God in Heaven what he would give to hold his Black Jack again, to feel the warm cozy burn of the rum as it washed down his parched throat. His tongue slathered across his lips at the thought. Even while he had been in Davy's grip, it was rum that he called for.

"Darby McGraw fetch aft the rum..."

But he'd never swallowed that last cup.

Bah. No sense reliving the past. He had this one night every year to visit the present era, not as a damned spirit, but once again as a Captain. He was still trapped inside of these four walls, but thanks to the witch's conjuring, on all Hallows Eve, he was granted flesh.

He opened the door and nearly bellowed when the noise reached his ears. Did they call that music now? A crew of drunken pirates sang better than the land-lubber who was belting out some horrific version of... Did he just sing "a pirate's life for me"?

His broad shoulders filled the narrow hallways as he turned into the Captain's Dining room. The source of the noise gripped a microphone, dancing and singing like a buffoon in a pirate costume. (He learned about those contraptions last Halloween.)

The Captain couldn't contain his growl of disgust. All eyes shifted toward him, sending a jolt of surprise from his head to his boot straps. They could see him. He had grown so accustomed to walking these rooms as a ghost, that it still shocked him to be noticed on this one night each year.

The singing pitiful-excuse-for-a-pirate stopped screaming into the noisemaker and slowly looked him over before facing the rest of the crowd again and announcing, "Great costume dude!"

The Captain glowered, and crossed his arms over his wide chest. "Best ye respect yer Captain, matey."

Uproarious laughter and applause was not the reaction he expected.

"Great accent, Buddy."

"Your costume looks amazing!"

The Captain frowned and stormed through the mob of useless fodder until he reached the more intimate dining room. One night was all he had. He didn't want to waste it with addle-minded chattel.

There was one person he wanted to see. She was worth waiting for.

He sat in one of the chairs, and drew the candelabra closer to him. His index finger slid back and forth through the tiny flame. He couldn't be burned. Not anymore. But this one night a year he could feel the heat, a miracle in itself.

While his finger danced in the candle's fire, he watched the entryway for any sign of her. He rolled his eyes when he saw what staggered through instead.

The drunken not-quite-a-pirate plopped down in a chair next to him and clapped his shoulder. "You've got the most killer Pirate costume I've ever seen. Where'd you get it?"

Before he could tell the faux pirate to take a walk off a short plank, his breath was stolen away by the raven-haired beauty he had been waiting for. Her eyes sparkled and her barely-there smile seared his cold soul.

Marie.

"Can I get you pirates some drinks?" She tossed down a couple of coasters shaped like hogshead rum barrels.

The Captain's mouth went dry at the sight of her, but sadly the man sitting next to him could still speak. The drunken would-be pirate's mouth contorted into a sloppy smile as he looked up at her. "Fetch us some grog, Wench!"

She rolled her eyes. "Look Blackbeard, I'm not dressed up as a pirate or a whore, so if you call me a wench one more time, I'll have to toss your ass out. Got it?"

He nodded and she winked at the Captain as she turned to head back to the kitchen.

The drunken sailor shook his head and blathered, "Wayfarin' wench workin' womanly wiles wherever she pleases, and then threatens me? I outta show her what happens to smart-mouthed wenches–"

His unconscious body dropped to the floor with a thud as the Captain wiped the blood from his ring.

"Pirates don' speak like that ye arse," he grumbled.

One punch. The Captain smiled. That felt

good.

Marie returned with two iced mugs of rum. She glanced around for the second pirate and then smiled. "Ok Flint. What'd you do with him?"

"Nothing that ye wouldn't have done, Lassie." He pointed to the floor. "He'll be sleepin' for a while."

She brought the mugs around and sat down beside him. "I've missed you."

He brought her hand up to his lips, pressing a tender kiss to her knuckles. Her skin smelled like heaven. Better than a westerly wind billowing the sails in to port.

"Aye. Tis a miracle to touch you again, Marie." He brought his hand up to cup her face, his calloused thumb caressing her cheek. "Yer smile is worth more to me than any treasure."

She laughed and shook her head. "You're a damned fine liar, Captain Flint."

"Tis no lie, my Beauty." He smiled and drew back from her, taking a swig of the rum. "So why did I rise to find drunken pirates singing in my house?"

"It's Halloween, remember? This year we added Karaoke night to the annual costume party."

He frowned. Although he haunted these walls every day, the future still passed him by on a regular basis. At times he felt like they spoke a different language. "Kara... Whatever it be called, is for singing?"

She took a sip of her mug and nodded. "Yep. We play music and they sing the song into the microphone. Anyone can do it."

"Aye, but some not so well." He glanced down at the unconscious pirate, then back to Marie. "Could I steal ye away from the party?"

Her smile could light the darkest storm. If his ancient heart still beat, it would be racing at the sight of her grin.

She nodded, "Of course. My shift was over this afternoon. I only stayed because I was waiting for you." She leaned forward and brushed a soft kiss to his cheek. "Let me put my apron away and I'll be right back."

He watched her go and lifted his mug again. He loved her more with each passing year. But while he watched her each day, relishing every smile, and aching with every frown, Marie couldn't see him. The rest of the year they couldn't touch. The only time she heard him during the rest of the year were the rare footfalls that sometimes sounded from his spirit-filled boots. Only on All Hallows Eve when the witch's curse transformed his ghostly body into flesh, could they truly be together.

How many more years would he still find her waiting for him?

He placed his empty mug back on the table. Rum simmered in his stomach, but the warmth didn't spread outward. He'd learned years ago that he could no longer feel the drunken effects of alcohol. But the taste was enough. A familiar comfort in a strange world that had left him behind as a myth in old pirate tales. Treasure Island. Bah!

Marie came back with a smile. He took her hand as they made their way outside to the covered porch. The salty night air filled his lungs with memories of an open ocean. He slid his arm around her waist and stared out into the darkness.

He searched the stars for the words to tell her how beautiful she looked and how much he wanted this night to last forever, but he came up empty. Simple words could never translate his feelings for her. Marie moved beside him, one hand sliding up to unfasten the buttons of his coat. Her soft fingers moved up his chest, searing his flesh with the warmth of her touch. He brought his hand up to rest over hers, pressing her palm to his heart.

"I remember the night we met. Ye weren't so eager to undress me then."

Marie laughed. "No I wasn't. I thought you were a kook!"

"I had to haunt ye for the next year before ye believed me to be the true Capn' Flint. Remember?"

"I do." She looked back out toward the Savannah coast. "I didn't believe the ghost stories of The Pirate's House. I didn't even know you were a real pirate. I thought Robert Louis Stevenson made you up for Treasure Island." She turned to meet his eyes again. "But then you started leaving me clues."

"Aye." He nodded. "How many years has it been now?"

She resumed loosening the ties on his shirt until her fingers slid inside against his cool flesh, drawing a deep throaty groan from his lips. He took her hands in his, halting her exploration of his chest.

"Ye did not answer my question, my Beauty."

Her eyes searched his and he felt his heart clench as a tear sparkled on her dark eyelash. "Flint, please. We only have a few hours."

He nodded. "Ye deserve better than this, Marie."

"A few hours with you is better than a lifetime with another man."

She wrenched her hands free of his grasp and tugged his collar, pulling him down until their lips met in a fevered, hungry kiss. He moaned against her lips, his resolve crumbling under the heat of their passion. His arms tightened around her small frame, clutching her to him. As her lips parted, he felt her gasping for air before their tongues caressed and wrestled to be even closer.

He could taste the rum on her lips as he lifted her up onto the railing. She wrapped her legs around his waist, her fingers tangling in the back of his thick dark hair.

Finally he drew back with a growl, resting his forehead against hers. "Gods Marie, I have no control around ye."

Her eyes sparkled. "Good."

She kissed him again, and he returned the affection. Tender, slow, long caresses, drinking her into his soul. How could he give her up? He couldn't. But was he selfish enough to let her waste her life away? He already lived his. Why couldn't he let her live hers?

Her fingernails slid up his back and fire scorched his soul. He gripped her tighter, carrying her back inside the Inn. He would never be strong enough to leave her. He needed her, wanted her.

He loved her.

Pulling back from their kiss he whispered, "Tell me where we can be alone."

"Upstairs," she answered against his neck.

As her legs slid down from his waist, he caught the back of her knees and swooped her up into his arms. He carried her up the back stairs and into one of the cordoned off bedrooms.

Kicking the door closed behind him, he carefully lowered her down onto the bed. Marie opened her arms to him. She was a vision with her raven hair fanned out over the white satin bedding. Her lips glistened, flushed from their passionate kisses, and her eyes shined up at him, beckoning him closer.

He stared down at her searching his soul for the strength to let her go, to send her back into the world of the living, but he was weak and selfish, and completely unable to resist the promise of her arms.

He lay down beside her and drew her into his embrace. Pressing a tender kiss to her silky hair, he whispered, "I love ye, Marie."

Her arms tightened around him as she pressed a kiss to his chest. "I love you too, Flint."

He lost himself in her, feeling her hands free him from his clothes while he explored every curve of her flesh. In the candlelight, sweat glistened on their bodies as they moved together. Their limbs tangled, until even their souls were entwined. When their passion reached its peak he drew back, his gaze locking with hers as he gasped her name. Her arms tightened around him along with the rest of her body, and he kissed her again, deeply, with every ounce of emotion that he carried in his ancient heart and soul.

Breathless, she pulled away, and he noticed her eyes shone with unshed tears.

"Why couldn't we have met before?" She whispered. "This isn't fair to love someone so much, and see him so little. We only get a few hours. I can't touch you or talk to you enough. I want to fall asleep in your arms and know that you'll be holding me when I wake up in the morning."

A tear spilled down her cheek and he kissed it away, tasting the salt on his lips. "Aye. Tis cruel this hand fate has dealt us, Love." He kissed her again and whispered, "Never have I loved as I love thee."

He met her eyes. "I love thee enough to let ye go, Marie. It will kill me not to see yer smile each day, but I am already long dead." Brushing her hair back from her forehead, he forced a tender smile. "My Beauty, ye are very much alive, and deserve a man who can love ye and treat ye like the priceless jewel ye are everyday, not just one night a year."

A sob escaped her rosy lips, and his heart broke at the sound. "I don't want anyone else, Flint. Knowing that you're there with me, watching me, even when I can't see you comforts me. It's enough."

He shook his head. "Not nearly enough."

"Stop it." She pushed at his chest. "Don't you dare try to tell me what's best for me."

He sighed and shifted off of her. Marie rolled on her side, resting her head on his chest as he stared up at the ceiling, his fingers absently sliding through her soft hair.

"I don' know what to do, Marie. I hurt ye if I go, and I hurt ye if I stay. I wish I could live again, to be the man ye need, but even if I could, I don' belong in this world filled with Kara..."

"Karaoke," she said. The soft chuckle in her voice soothed him.

"Right. Where would an old salt like Capn' Flint fit into this world?"

Silence fell over them and in his mind he could hear a phantom clock ticking away their precious minutes together.

Marie lifted her head to look down at him, wiping away her tears with a determined smile. "This sucks, Flint."

"Aye." He brought his hand up to cup her soft cheek. She was a vision. His angel.

His. Yet not.

"Any chance that witch would come back and give you flesh more often?"

Flint laughed, he couldn't help himself. That was yet another of Marie's gifts. She was a ray of sunshine in his darkness even when he was certain he may never see the sun again.

"I think she is long dead, Love. She didn't know what she had done anyway. She was only tryin' to make contact with me. Never knew she got her incantation wrong."

"Well maybe this year I'll find some sort of

time machine and go back to 1745 and stop you from drinking so much rum. We could be alive together, at the same time."

He chuckled and shook his head. "Those days were not kind, Love. I wouldn't want ye to have to live through that."

Her smile faded away as her voice lowered to a whisper. "Then there's only one solution."

"Solution?"

"Kill me."

His eyes widened. "What? That be no solution, Marie! No!"

"Just hear me out. I'm growing older, dying slowly every day anyway. I want to be with you. I don't have any family here or obligations. No one would miss me."

Flint sat upright, taking her with him as he held her shoulders, forcing her to meet his gaze. "Ye don' know what yer askin' Love. To be a ghost, haunting these walls is no life. It's a curse. An' I would never bring it upon ye. Never."

"You told me once before you can see the other ghosts that are trapped here. We could see each other. Don't you see? I'd never get old. We could be together now and always. That's not a curse. It's an end to one."

He rubbed his calloused hands down his face, fighting the temptation of her argument. With a sigh, he met her eyes again. "Don' ask me to take yer life, Marie. Please. This is not our answer."

She took his hand and he stared down at her slender fingers against his sea-weathered knuckles. Giving his hand a squeeze she kissed his cheek.

"I'm sorry, Flint. I just hate being apart from you. There has to be a way to be together."

"Aye, I wish it were so, but maybe this was never meant to be. Tis probably why the living cannot see the dead. We have no future together."

"Don't say that." She wiped a stray tear. "Please. Your love is the best thing that ever happened to me."

Pulling her back into his arms, he rested his cheek on her head, closing his eyes and breathing in the scent of her hair. Memorizing every sensation, every caress, every curve, bracing himself for another year of seeing her without being able to talk, or touch, or smell, or taste. Another year of being a spirit trapped in The Pirate's House Inn.

She sighed and pulled back from his arms. "How can the night already be over?"

He looked at the clock, his heart clutching at the time. "We still have the better part of an hour, Love."

"Just give me a second, ok?"

He watched her disappear in the bathroom, and when she returned she wore only an oversized captain's coat and a smile. He raised a brow with a crooked smile of approval.

"I thought you might like it. It's a replica of yours. We had it stashed in the bathroom here so the Halloween party-goers weren't tempted to try it on."

"It looks perfect on ye, my Love."

She got back in bed beside him, pulling him down to kiss her again. He hummed at the feel of her cool lips against his. Apparently she'd brushed her teeth while she was gone too. He could taste the mint covering the flavor of rum.

After they made love again, she drifted off to sleep in his arms. He stared down at her, watching her sleep as the morning light started to filter through the window. He reached up to touch her hair as his fingers gradually became translucent. He couldn't feel her skin any longer. Their night was over. He growled in frustration, knowing he wouldn't wake her.

She could no longer hear his voice.

"Lord why do ye curse me so? Why bring our paths to cross only to deny us? She wanted me to kill her tonight, for Godssake! What am I to do?"

"Just love me."

He jumped back and gasped when Marie sat up.

Only she didn't sit up. Her body was still

lying on the bed. His brow furrowed as he met her eyes again. "Are ye dreaming, Lass? How can this be?"

She looked over her shoulder at her sleeping body and back to his eyes. "I broke the curse."

"What? How?"

She reached out and took his hand. He felt her touch. His gaze snapped from their hands to her face and then back to her sleeping form on the bed. Gradually he met her eyes.

"If I couldn't live in your arms," she whispered. "Then I wanted to die there."

He shook his head with tears in his eyes and reached up to caress her cheek. "What have ye done?"

"I was pretty sure you wouldn't kill me when I asked, but I didn't know if I'd be brave enough to do it myself. I stashed some sleeping pills in the bathroom and mixed them with rum. I'm sorry I couldn't tell you, but I was afraid you'd try to stop me."

"Aye, I would have." He shook his head. "Twas a crazy chance ye took. What if ye were wrong? What if yer spirit had gone? I would have lost ye forever."

"It was a chance I had to take. I couldn't face another year without you. I've thought about this for a long time. I knew what I wanted."

He scooped her up into his arms and carried her out of the room. Someone would find her body soon enough, and he didn't want to be there to see them zip her in a bag and carry her out like unwanted garbage.

Once they were downstairs, he lowered her to the ground and smiled as he looked down into her eyes. "I hope ye never regret yer choice, my Love."

"The chance to spend forever with my favorite pirate? Never."

He grinned in spite of himself. "I be yer *only* pirate, Lass!"

She laughed and his heart soared. "Maybe my only Captain."

"Ye be a terrible liar, my Beauty!" He raised a playful brow and inside his soul wept for joy. He'd been alone for so long. To be able to laugh and smile, and touch, was a priceless gift. His grin softened as he whispered, "Ye be my greatest Treasure, Marie."

She answered him with the most perfect kiss he'd ever received on this or any side of eternity.

The End

1530 Archibald Street

October. The night encroached on the sunshine, stealing time from the day. A chill crept through the air as shadows lengthened. Dried husks of leaves dropped to the ground, and summer silently faded away.

The wind moaned through thinning trees, naked branches scratched against window panes. Homework beckoned the children indoors, leaving the streets eerily silent while the nocturnal creatures ventured further out from their hiding places.

Burt lived at 1521 Archibald Street. An average street in an average town. His home consisted of two bedrooms, two bathrooms, and a tiny detached garage. He lived alone since his wife became his ex-wife, but he was comfortable. Just he, and his dog, Champ.

It started off like a typical Wednesday night. American Idol was back for a new season, and Burt parked himself on his worn sofa with Champ curled up at the other end.

During the commercial break, he glanced over at his companion with a sigh. "Hey buddy, want to help me take out the trash?"

Champ lifted his mostly gray face, then groaned and placed his head back onto his paws. His heavy lids closed as if he'd never been interrupted from his nap.

"Fine." Burt grumbled and got up. "Must be nice to live a dog's life."

He pulled on a hooded sweatshirt and hustled out to the side of the garage to grab his trash can. Some things never changed. Every Wednesday night he pulled the trash can to the curb and every Thursday he brought the empty can back to the side of the garage.

Taking out the trash was one of the few things that remained constant after Tami left him.

The wheels of the trash can clamored up the cracked cement of his driveway, silencing the crickets and coyote howls. With the full moon lighting his path, he avoided tripping over the uneven concrete and settled the can at the edge of his driveway. Burt started to turn back toward his house, but something caught his eye.

A single trash can sat outside the crooked gate of the old Granger place.

The hair rose on the back of Burt's neck.

1530 Archibald Street was empty. Forgotten.

Or so he thought.

While Burt stood contemplating, he had no idea he was being watched, lusted after, yearned for.

Foreboding twisted his gut, but he convinced himself to move forward. He told himself it was just kids messing around. Halloween was tomorrow night. Maybe some teens were starting the spook party early? As he got closer to the weather-beaten house a breeze tickled the back of his neck sending a chill down the length of his spine.

Burt stopped, staring at the abandoned house, never realizing the house was staring right back at him.

The Granger place had been abandoned for years. Over time stories were whispered about curses and evil spirits. Tales were spun of murders, missing persons, missing pets, and of course ghosts and ancient burial grounds, but Burt didn't believe the rumors. He figured the Granger place was a victim of foreclosure and a soft real estate market, not curses.

The house liked that about Burt.

When he reached the lone trash can, he spun around. He couldn't see anything, but he felt it. In the distance, he could hear Champ's muffled barking. The commercials were probably over. He should get back home.

The trash can toppled over.

The house waited.

Burt frowned and bent to lift the can when he noticed a copy of the local newspaper on top. It wasn't the sight of the paper that caught his eye. It was the date. November 1st 1950. The picture showed a pristine new home with a manicured lawn surrounding a fountain with a headline that read "Welcome Home."

1530 Archibald hadn't looked like that picture in years.

Dropping the paper back into the can, Burt glanced up at the house. The arched windows on either side of the door gave the illusion of eyes. The peeling paint showed the Granger place's age, and the fountain was long dry, the top tier chipped and broken.

Without realizing it, Burt stepped closer to the dilapidated gate. Rust had eaten through the top hinge, so the one-time-barrier now hung listless at a precarious angle. But it wasn't the gate that made Burt forget about his Wednesday night date with American Idol.

It was the yard on the other side.

The landscaping was dead, brown and crispy, and yet, perfectly manicured. Not a single stray leaf littered the expanse of crunchy lawn. In the moonlight, he couldn't be sure, but it almost looked as though the yard was raked.

A loud thud followed by the scraping sound of a broom caught his attention.

"Is someone there?" Burt gave out a half-hearted call.

The house creaked in answer as a gust of wind moaned through the trees.

He gripped the gate, lifting and pulling. The rusted hinge squealed in protest drowning out Champ's panicked howling and barking. Burt told himself he had to be sure some kids weren't jumping off the roof in the backyard. All he needed was to be awakened by fire trucks and ambulances in the middle of the night.

The house sat hungry. Waiting.

Dead brittle grass crunched under his worn tennis shoes as he called out again. "Is anybody there?"

Burt started to feel foolish, when he heard another metallic clatter that stopped him in his tracks. His brow furrowed. "If you don't come out, I'm callin' the police. This is private property."

The house was well-aware of that fact.

A man rounded the far corner of the house with a rake and shovel and a wide-brimmed straw hat, as if the moonlight might burn his skin.

"Hey there. You got permission to be on this property?"

Burt could see the man's hat nodding in the affirmative, but he didn't answer, just went to work, raking non-existent leaves and digging out water-wells around the dead hedge as if it might see water again sometime soon.

"This yard awful dry, don't you think?" Burt called out.

The house needed more than water, but it kept quiet as its minion worked the immaculate dead landscaping.

Burt frowned, wanting to go home, but instead found himself inexplicably moving closer to the yard worker. "Did you hear me?"

Now that he stood only a couple of feet away from the man, he noticed the yard worker wore dusty old black and white wing-tipped shoes, and his pants were actually slacks riddled with moth-holes.

What kind of man did yard work at night, in a dead yard, wearing their grandfather's clothes out of the attic? Burt wondered.

He frowned and asked again, "Did you hear me?"

The hat bobbed up and down.

"So why don't you answer me?"

The hat tilted back as the yard worker finally made eye contact.

But he had no eyes.

Burt screamed as the eyeless minion leapt forward, closing the distance between them. Burt found himself wrapped in an inescapable vise-like embrace until his rib snapped, pain stealing his voice.

The hinges squeaked as the front door opened to a chasm of darkness.

Burt struggled, digging his heels into the dry ground, but the minion lugged him closer, tugging him up the first step of the porch.

"Let me go! I won't tell anyone about you, just leave me be."

The minion opened his mouth to answer, moaning and grunting in an effort to construct words. Burt suddenly realized his eyes weren't the only thing missing.

"Dear god," he gasped.

His captor had no tongue.

Burt closed his eyes and slammed his head back into the disfigured yard worker. Stars erupted at the edge of his vision, but the eyeless man loosened his grip long enough for Burt to scramble free. Clutching his injured side, he stumbled toward the stairs, but before he could step down, the stairs vanished from sight. Burt hit the ground, his ankle turning at a strange angle until he felt something pop.

In spite of the pain, he rolled onto his belly, desperate to crawl to safety.

He never saw the eyeless man raising his shovel.

The hollow crack of the shovel left Burt motionless in front of the house. Quickly the minion brought the prey to his master and the house closed its door behind them.

Deep within the walls the house fed. And plotted.

Outside, the fountain in front of 1530 Archibald Street burst to life.

Tomorrow, Halloween would bring teenagers looking for a thrill.

And the house would be ready.

Ready and waiting.

The End… Or is it?

The Caretaker

I love her. I hate her.

Her beauty drew me into her circle, and I have been trapped here ever since. The years fly by, but my hair doesn't gray, my face doesn't change. All those I once loved are lost to me. Probably dead, but I don't know for certain. I haven't seen them since the foggy All Hallow's Eve when I stumbled out into the darkness and heard her song. I've lost count of the years we've been together.

The mist was thick, and the night was ripe for a storm when I found her. I could smell the rain, although the skies had yet to release a drop.

Haunting melodies from a calliope danced on the chilly night wind. I'd never heard anything so wickedly lovely. Following the chimes of the song, I ventured further out into the darkness.

My muscles ached as I held my heavy iron lantern out in front of me, lighting my path. When I finally saw the horses circling in the distance, I thought I was dreaming. Never before had I seen anything so beautiful.

The fog thinned in the meadow and the moonlight shimmered through, shining down on elaborate painted horses spinning and dancing to the music piped out from the center. A carousel. I'm not sure how many miles I walked that night, but after passing through a village I didn't recognize, I heard my mother's warning in my head.

Every time you find yourself in a new town you have to shore up your defenses, Duffy. Shore them up tight, because you could run into the Devil Himself or his top salesman...

My name is Duffy Grimmod, the Devil's top salesman.

I'm actually the barker for a Victorian carousel.

Her carousel.

She is the only silver grey horse on the circle. She's also the only horse that has life in her eyes. Hunger. And every year I help her feed. I call her Stormy. Her real name is Scelestus, but it's tough to pronounce when you are enticing riders to forget their worries and climb aboard.

She takes them for the ride of their lives. Their last ride.

You see, every Halloween, her carousel grows. Behind every fiery steed is a story. Some were runaways, lost souls searching for sanctuary, while others were cocky teens who should have listened to the fear that gnawed at their gut. We even have a couple of horses who were young mothers looking for an escape.

Stormy chooses them, and I help them aboard and start the calliope.

And I am tired.

I've tried to escape her clutches more than once, but she holds my soul in her grasp. I guess by now you know she is much more than she seems. I hear her velvet voice, drenching her wishes in a sugar I cannot resist, and venom I dare not defy. I serve her year after year, and always her carousel grows.

Most riders aren't chosen to stay, only the ones who ride on Stormy's back. She can be very picky. Over the years, I've learned that she looks for a certain type of soul. Rich or poor, ugly or beautiful, angry or angelic, none of that seems to matter. It's a yearning she searches for in each soul. Those are the ones she calls to ride.

I can see the need in their eyes, the wonder when they touch her saddle. On some level, they understand this ride will change their life forever. Most riders climb up without my intervention, but occasionally they sense something. Fear creeps in.

They know.

Before they can get down, I ring the bell and the flying horses lurch into motion. With each spin of her circular spell, I watch the life drain from their eyes. Faster and faster the horses run. Lights sparkle in the mirrored center, as the garish steeds spin and the calliope drowns out the squeals and laughter.

And the screams.

I don't know if the transformation is painful, but I have witnessed too many silent cries amidst the joy that permeates the carousel. Their souls are drained and their bodies mutate and harden, until they are finally a permanent part of her wicked ride. Over the years, I have saved two riders from her appetite.

She only punished me once.

That was the night of my last escape attempt.

Her name was Nan. She heard the pipes calling to her and followed their song. When she stepped out from the shadows and into the dancing lights of the carousel, she took center stage in my heart. I'd never felt anything like it.

At once I heard the sweet call from Stormy. *Bring her*, she whispered into my mind.

I glanced over at her, her silver coat forever shining under the bright, twinkling lights, ribbons blowing back on a phantom wind no one else could feel. Her yellow eyes glittered, the only sign that she was more than she seemed.

I answered her with a shake of my head.

Her call persisted. *Bring her to me, Duffy.*

Instead I walked toward the woman, tipping my hat as I approached. "Good Evenin' Miss. Name's Duffy, can I help you?"

Nan pulled her eyes from the carousel for a moment and smiled. My heart clenched. I couldn't let her touch Stormy. That was probably exactly why the demon horse wanted her.

"I'm Nan. I heard the music, and I had to see where it came from."

I nodded. I'd heard that story before. For many people those were the last words they ever said.

"I'm sorry if the music woke you. I'm just closing down for the night."

Duffy! Stormy bellowed in my mind, making me wince a bit. *I called this one. She is for me. Bring her to me.*

"The horses are beautiful," Nan said, taking a few more steps toward Stormy. "I'd love to have a ride."

I moved in front of her, blocking her path. "Maybe tomorrow. We're closed now."

Suddenly without my help, the carousel sang, and the horses lurched into action. Damn her!

Nan rose up on her tip toes, peering around my shoulders, her eyes sparkled as she watched the spectacle behind me. "Maybe just one time around before you close?"

"No." I took her elbow and guided her away. "There's some sort of malfunction. It's been starting and stopping like that all night. I couldn't have you getting hurt on my watch, now could I?"

For the first time since she walked into the light of the carousel, she looked up at me. Really looked. The spell was broken. I smiled and kept walking with her. "I could sure use a bite to eat. Can you recommend anyplace around here?"

We shared a meal at the only burger joint open late. I couldn't remember the last time I had eaten. Stormy's magic sustained me. When I walked Nan home, she gave me a gentle kiss on the cheek that set my soul on fire.

"I hope I see you again, Duffy," she said.

"I hope so too. Goodnight, Nan."

I watched her go inside and turned to leave when I realized that I really did want to see her again. I didn't want to polish brass carousel poles or dust the horses anymore. I didn't want to keep the prison for lost souls shiny and enticing.

I couldn't watch another life fade away.

Instead of returning to the field where Stormy waited, I walked in the opposite direction. I didn't have any money, but I could sleep in a stairwell and look for work in the morning. For the first time in decades, I felt free. I had choices, and none of them would take a life. I smiled, but something dripped from my chin.

When I reached up and wiped it away, my fingers were covered in blood.

I gasped when I realized my hands were bleeding too. My skin was paper thin and cracking.

Return to me, Duffy. Return or die.

Stormy! I clenched my fists, but the moment the muscles in my forearms contracted, I felt my skin split open. More blood oozed through the fabric of my shirt, my skin melting away like my body was made of candle wax.

Panic rose inside, and my instinct to live overpowered my stubborn wish to die. I turned back and stumbled toward Stormy, toward the carousel of the damned. I caught my reflection in the orange glow of the gaslamps along the street. My hair was white, my skin sallow and shriveled. I was finally my true age.

Stormy's spell was weakening.

I was dying.

Hurry Duffy.

I lumbered through the streets, the brittle bones in my feet snapping with each step. I groaned in pain, unable to scream because my vocal chords could no longer produce a tone. I could feel decayed flesh oozing from my arms and legs like honey, but still I struggled. When I finally saw the lights in the distance, they were mottled, disfigured by the milky haze of my cataract-filled eyes.

I crumbled at her feet, her frozen hooves poised above my head. I wanted to be courageous. I wanted to spit on the polished wood floor of the carousel and tell her to let me die.

Instead I wept and begged for my pitiful existence.

The carousel came to life, spinning until it vanished from the field, but Stormy left me in my condition for days. I drowned in an ocean of pain until she finally restored me.

You are the chosen one, Duffy. My caretaker. You will care for me until I choose another. Your life is mine.

I was so grateful for the pain to end, for my vision to be restored, my voice, and even my hair, that for a few years I enticed riders without thought or pity on their souls. A selfish indulgence on my part, but until you've suffered the indescribable pain she put me through, you can't understand.

I stood by and let the calliope sing out on the Halloween wind, calling to those seekers, enticing them to ride, to toss their cares aside.

But that was years ago.

The pain of my last escape has dulled. I am tired. Each time we appear on Halloween, I polish her saddle, shine the ribbons on her bridle, and I pray I will find my replacement. No one ever measures up. But I keep searching. She wants someone who people will trust, who will bring her more riders.

Someone like *you*, perhaps.

You heard the call this Hallows Eve night. The calliope melody put a song into your soul that sent you searching for us. Now you see the beauty, spinning before you.

You see your reflection in her eyes, don't you? You want an escape. Are you tired of the problems you face at work? Have you exhausted yourself looking for the right mate, or the right job? Do you ever wish you could walk away from it all? Do you wish life could be a fairy tale filled with white horses and music?

Maybe you're the one I've been searching for.

Come closer and have a look at the silver mare on the edge. Yes, she's the one. Did you see her eyes sparkle?

She likes you, my friend. Can you hear her calling your name? You can; I can see it on your face. Your name has never sounded as sweet as it does when Stormy calls for you.

I might even miss her calling mine. Maybe.

But don't mind me. Please, step right up and take a ride...

The ride of your life.

For your life.

Happy Halloween.

The End

The Third King

The sand blew against their veiled faces, stinging their eyes as the caravan trudged countless miles through the desert. The three kings, mounted on camels, rode on through the darkness, guided only by the light of a single bright star in the night sky.

He had become one of them, a mysterious, learned Magus, one of Persia's elite Magi Kings. He rode among them, veiled; not to protect his face from the blowing sand, but to hide his hardened, immortal skin from the eyes of the mortals around him.

The tall dark man the mortals called Balthasar, could sense the growing dissension within the caravan. From atop his camel, he could hear their hushed whispers. They believed their Kings had gone mad. No wise man would wander the barren desert, following a star, just to see a newborn baby. There had been moments during their journey when their quest did seem like madness, but they were committed.

They had come too far to turn back now.

The previous night, the Magi had stood before King Herod and told him of the star that had brought them to his kingdom. They had traveled from Persia to see the ancient prophecy fulfilled, and asked the monarch where the baby lay so they might see this "King of Kings". Herod explained the prophecy that a child would be born in the town of Bethlehem. Herod had not yet found the child, and he urged the three Magi Kings to search diligently for the infant. Upon finding the babe, he asked the Magi Kings to send word to him so he might also pay homage to this "chosen one".

Balthasar stared at Herod with immortal eyes that had witnessed centuries of treachery. He blinked slowly and opened his mind, allowing the human thoughts to reach him. It was plain to see Herod plotted to slaughter the child.

Balthasar felt his ancient pulse quicken. Mighty King Herod feared a newborn infant. Could this child they crossed the barren desert to find truly be the son of God? Was he witnessing an act of a supreme being, of the Creator himself? Balthasar had to know...

They left Herod's kingdom, and he rode on in silence, listening to the undercurrent of gossip among the caravan with inhuman ears. Men had been disappearing along their journey from Persia to Herod's throne, and finally, to Bethlehem. The others assumed the missing men had abandoned the mission across the desert and fled back to Persia, but had they been able to see beneath the sand, they would have found many bloodless bodies along their route. Balthasar's immortality came at a very high price.

It didn't matter. He had no need for grooms and servants and cooks, and, in fact, had no real need for his camel, although riding did help him to hide his pronounced limp. He shifted his body slightly, finding the camel saddle to be extremely uncomfortable.

"Do you require another pillow, my master?" An attentive young servant called up to him.

He waved the boy off, refusing his offer; as he instinctively reached down to touch his lower leg. Feeling the cool porcelain limb still in its proper place, the King urged his camel onward. The excitement grew within him with each passing hour as he neared the end of this journey, neared the fulfillment of perhaps the greatest prophecy ever foretold. If the Jewish prophets were correct, then he was about to look into the eyes of God incarnate!

How he wished he could share this moment with his maker. She had an inquiring mind, and spent centuries in search of philosophical truths. He knew she would have been eager to join him in this quest. With the rise of the Jews in Egypt, he and his maker had spent countless hours debating the reality of a single God. They had stood and watched the gods of the Egyptians, the Greeks, and the Romans fall, and yet they still had never found answers. She could debate nightly until the sun rose.

Oh how he missed hearing her ideas on philosophy and religion, but that was lifetimes ago...

As the Kings traveled on through the night, his mind drifted back to his mortal days in Egypt. As a young man, he had been a soldier for his Pharaoh until the battle which cost him his lower leg. He survived his wounds, but over the years he lost the inner-struggle with bitterness. Angry and disgusted with his deformity, he became a sharp-tongued servant, traded from household to household until the day he saw her. Her hair was as dark as coal with warm brown eyes that masked her intelligence behind their sultry, mysterious beauty.

He had never met a woman like her before. Maybe he never would again. Her knowledge of politics and philosophy intrigued him, and after speaking with her for only a few brief minutes, he had known he would be her loyal servant until his death.

His promise was fulfilled through years of faithful service. He never dreamed she would repay him with eternal life.

But then he hadn't known his Mistress was a vampire. He still missed her, and thought of her often, but it was impossible for him to return. She already had a mate, and he loved her far too much to spend eternity watching her love another man.

He was known as Bomani when he left Egypt to travel the world. He journeyed far north, until he reached the distant land of Persia, where he began training as a Magus. He spent countless hours night after night voraciously reading, learning and teaching others until his reputation gained him favor with a wealthy Lord in the desert land. The Lord had been unsuccessful in conquering nearby nomadic tribes and begged for Bomani's assistance. Using his strategic plans, the Lord reclaimed his lands from the nomads, and upon their victory, he gratefully bestowed upon Bomani a new Persian name. He granted him a noble title meaning, War Advisor. Bomani became, Balthasar.

Upon the monarch's death, he bequeathed the rule of his small kingdom to the much-admired magus. Soon, Balthasar became a benevolent ruler, adored by all who lived within his reign. Always careful to keep his face veiled, no mortal ever laid eyes on his ageless flesh.

Many years passed before the news reached him that Moses had led the Jews to freedom from slavery in Egypt. Having been a servant during his mortal life, he too, believed every man should be free, but the thought of the cosmos being created by a single omnipotent God, as the Jews claimed, seemed preposterous to him at the time.

In his opinion, the world was too complex to be the work of one single being. Over the centuries, there were many Jewish prophets who talked of a coming Messiah, and although Balthasar did not practice this religion, the Magi in his country always strived to gain knowledge of the spiritual as well as the physical world. When prophecies of different religions reached his kingdom, Balthasar kept record of them.

Decades later, he awoke to find the night sky aglow as the heavens parted to welcome a single star's beam of light. The light shone directly onto him, casting his silhouette over the desert sands. He stood in awe of the strange light, finally wondering if this might be the sign from Jehovah that the Jewish prophets predicted.

Quickly the Magi came together to discuss this blazing sign they saw glowing above. Determined to understand the star's true meaning, Melchior, Caspar and Balthasar vowed to follow the star's light. Within hours, they had the caravan loaded and set out on their journey to seek out 'the one born to be King'.

Many weeks had passed since they left Persia, and tonight their journey would reach its end. Balthasar could see the star's light had stopped ahead of them, shining down on the rooftop of a small house in the town of Bethlehem. As the neared the house, Balthasar's brow furrowed. The star shone not on a home, but a small barn for farm animals.

Could this truly be the birthplace of a mighty king?

The night was too quiet, almost deafening in its silence. Even the wind no longer moaned around them.

The Magi dismounted their camels and looked at one another without speaking a word, sensing the sound could break the spell. Balthasar could feel magic surround him as he collected his gift for the child, and silently he wondered how he would know if this was truly the "Christ Child" that filled so many of the Hebrew prophecies.

Servants quickly surrounded him, draping royal robes over his windblown linens. Finally, two more servants approached the dark veiled King as he knelt to receive his crown. After placing it on his head, the servants bowed, whispering praises to their ruler as they retreated back to the caravan.

Balthasar gazed down at his appearance. It still stunned him to see his royal turnout. He had been Bomani, a slave for most of his mortal life, and at times he still felt like that servant of long ago, not the Magi King of this night.

He took a deep breath, and, clutching his gift of gold, he approached Melchior and Caspar. He didn't know them well, but he knew they were very committed and learned Magi Kings. They too longed to know if this child was indeed the Son of God.

The three Kings nodded to one another and slowly entered the stable. Nothing could have prepared Balthasar for the scene he found. He could sense a tangible love filling the stall, touching and surrounding all who entered. The animals were alert, but stood eerily still and silent as Balthasar quietly gazed at the mother of this infant king.

He looked into her mind and found her name was Mary. Her face radiated a pure beauty unlike anything he had ever seen. With her long dark hair pulled back, she looked up toward her husband with deep adoration. Peace and contentment embraced her, and the longer Balthasar stood before the child's mother, the more her mind opened to him.

His hands trembled when he realized that although she had given birth to a son, Mary had never laid with her husband, or any mortal man. The woman seated before him, the mother of this Chosen One, was a virgin.

Impossible, and yet...

Balthasar forced his eyes from her face, and turned his silent attention toward her husband, Joseph. He was a tall man with dark brown curled locks of hair. His hands were hardened from years of hard labor.

The Magi King easily read from his mind that he was a carpenter, and although all of his family and acquaintances insisted Mary had disgraced him, this humble man bravely upheld her honor and stood beside her. He believed he had seen an Angel of God who proclaimed he would name his wife's son, Jesus...

"The babe would be the Son of God..." The thought echoed through Balthasar's mind.

Gradually he let his vampiric eyes fall onto the baby lying in the manger. This was not an ordinary child. This baby did not cry, and Balthasar could see wisdom in the child's eyes.

And there was something else.

A light emanated from this infant; an aura of light so pure it penetrated into even the darkest of souls.

"It was this child," His mind whispered. The magic, the love, the peace he had felt when he entered the stable was all here in the babe lying before him. The emotions pouring over and through him had been coming from the child!

He stared at the baby and suddenly felt the hair on the back of his neck begin to rise. When the child met his eyes he heard a voice speak directly into his mind.

Balthasar.

He fell to his knees and bowed his head, hiding the deep red blood tears falling from his eyes. He was unworthy to see such a miracle! Without a word, Balthasar offered up his gift of gold, an eternal metal symbolizing the eternal king. He felt Mary lift the weight from his hands, as he remained at the manger with his head bowed.

He chanted a silent prayer until he heard the voice in his mind once more.

You have been brought here by God to save his only son. You are a most worthy servant, Balthasar, for as you are now a king, you were once a slave. In my Father's kingdom the meek shall inherit the earth, and the servant shall be served.

Then the voice went silent. Balthasar could

feel his body tremble as he rose up to look at the innocent child wrapped in swaddling clothes.

The baby glowed, bathed in the warm light of the bright star that led the Magi to his cradle; his beauty was indescribable. All of the gods the ancient vampire worshiped hungered for riches and sacrifice. They were powerful, vengeful and vain, but this child bundled in a manger lay vulnerable, defenseless and innocent.

If the Hebrew prophecies were truly the word of God, then this was like no God Balthasar had ever known. This was a God who loved his creation so much he chose to come down from the heavens and walk among his people as one of them.

Balthasar averted his eyes, suddenly ashamed to look upon the babe. How could he, a blood drinker and child of the night, deserve this God's love? Had this God of the Jews really called to him? Could his journey across the desert be part of a divine plan?

He forced his eyes up one last time to look upon the child before rising to stand. The star had led them to meet King Herod, and then to find this baby, all in the dark of night. The one time he was able to walk the earth...

Balthasar stood slowly, knowing now why he had been brought to this place to see this miracle. He approached Joseph and nodded in greeting.

"Glad tidings to you, Joseph. I have been given a sign from God to warn you. King Herod wishes to slay this child. He fears your babe is the child the prophets foretold would grow to overpower him and take his throne. You must take Mary and the child away from this land and into Egypt. Use our gifts to finance the journey, but make haste. Herod may already be searching for you."

He turned to face Caspar and Melchior, and the three Magi Kings slowly exited the small stable. They decided each king would take a different route to return to their homelands so Herod would not be able to question them on the location of the Chosen One.

Balthasar watched as the caravan dispersed. He sent his grooms and servants with Melchior and Caspar. He would no longer need them.

Instead, the mysterious Magus turned and walked alone toward the south, toward his ancient home of Egypt. With each step, he removed a royal garment until he remained clothed only in a slave's white robe as he walked through the darkness. The Magus King, Balthasar, was no more.

Bomani moved quickly as the blowing desert sands stung his uncovered face. Finally he stopped and looked up into the night sky, weeping tears of joy for the knowledge he was no longer alone in his endless night. He had a purpose.

"You gave us your gift of love in darkness, that even we, who live only in the dark of night, might see your light..."

Centuries have gone by since that night, and each year a dark stranger still walks through the same sands to the place where a stable once stood. The bright light of a single star shines down, silhouetting his thin frame on the sand. Alone and silent, he stands, looking up into the starlight, hoping one day there will be an end to his wandering.

Waiting for the day when the child he saw so many centuries ago will finally bring his servant home.

The End

The Business Trip

Traveling to Los Angeles made his ancient bones ache. Poverty and avarice commingled in this city of angels, and the sight of so many broken dreams weighed on his heart.

Outside the brightly lit stores, tireless volunteers rang their bells, reminding the shoppers of less fortunate families without coins for food, let alone shiny new gifts to rest under their non-existent tree.

Out of the corner of his eye, he noticed a shopper hustling out of a store. Before he could leap out of the way, she slammed into him and they both crumpled into a heap on the sidewalk.

"Are you all right?" She struggled to get up so he could breathe. "I'm sorry. I didn't see you..." She scanned both sides of the street while he got to his feet. Her brow furrowed. "Where's your Mom?" Her eyes met his. "You're not out here alone tonight, are you?"

He sighed. "I'm much older than I look."

"Are you sure you're not hurt?"

He nodded and held out his hand. "I'm fine. My name is Leon."

"Nice to meet you, Leon. I'm Grace." She gripped his hand and he smiled. With a single touch, he knew the shopper was a single Mom with two little ones at home. Her cousin was watching them while she shopped for the few gifts she could afford. She didn't have much money for Christmas shopping, but she was happy to have a gift for each of them.

It was also apparent she wasn't the reason for his business trip to the human world.

"Merry Christmas." He released her hand and smiled. Part of him wished he could see her face when she got home and unloaded her bags to find extra gifts of roadrunner footed pajamas for her young son, and a new art set for her daughter.

"Merry Christmas." She checked once more for any sign of another adult. "I don't want to leave out here on your own. Do you know your Mom's cell phone number? I could call her for you."

"Thank you, Grace, but I assure you my height is misleading."

"Oh you're a..." Her cheeks flushed with color as she swallowed her words.

"I'm a little person."

"I'm sorry. I didn't mean to offend you."

He shook his head. "Not at all. I hope you and your young ones have a wonderful Christmas."

He turned and walked away before her inevitable questions started. He hadn't meant to let it slip that he knew about her children. It was a rookie mistake, and he was well past that stage in his profession.

When he rounded the corner, the shadows grew. Without the well-lit storefronts, the yellowed streetlights barely kept the night at bay. He pulled his jacket tighter, and underneath his knit cap, the points of his ears twitched.

Across the street, someone squashed an aluminum can. He turned and headed toward the noise. As he approached, the night went silent. He squinted into the darkness.

"Is anyone there?" He took another step into the shadows. "I won't hurt you."

"I'm calling 911," a timid voice answered.

"All right."

"All right?"

Leon shrugged. "I guess so. Who is 911?"

After a moment, he saw a bag lady step out of the shadows. "You don't know 911? The police are there."

"At 911?"

"Yes." She took another step closer and he realized she wasn't as old as he thought. "They drive by here sometimes. Their cars are pretty." A faint smile haunted her dirty features. "They light up like Christmas."

He hadn't touched her yet, so her human life was still a mystery, but it was obvious from looking at her that she didn't deserve the life she was living.

"My name is Leon. I came here to help you."

Her brow creased as if she was seeing him for the first time. Gradually her frown transformed into a most angelic smile.

Could this girl must be the reason for his business trip? Walking down the alleyway hadn't been a premeditated choice; he let his heart take the lead.

She took a tentative step forward. "Your name is Noel."

His jaw went slack for a moment before he cleared his throat. "Excuse me?"

Her eyes sparkled even in the dim lighting. "You're an elf." She glanced around and lowered her voice. "Don't worry no one would believe me anyway. They all think I'm crazy."

"They?"

"Everyone." She shrugged, and her smile vanished.

Her gaze went vacant and he wondered what she saw. Without meaning to, he reached out to take her cold hand in his. Her short life flashed in his mind and he closed his eyes. How many more times would he be forced to bear witness to the underbelly of this world?

There wasn't enough Christmas magic left to bring the spirit of the season back, especially not in this city. Each time he was sent out to restore hope and good cheer, he lost a little more of his ancient soul to bitterness. The city snuffed out any sparks of joy.

She shook her head and squeezed his hand. "Sorry Noel. I didn't mean to space out. Come with me."

Without waiting for an answer, she tugged his hand, rushing through the catacombs of back alleys. He had to run to keep up with her. When they reached an abandoned factory, she slowed down thrumming her fingertips along the chain link fence.

"I have a secret opening. It keeps us safe."

"Us?"

She glanced back at him and smiled. "You'll see, Noel."

How did she know his real name? He always turned it backward when he crossed into the human world. But somehow she knew. It made no sense. She was human. He could tell that much from holding her hand. Another teen lost in the town full of false promises.

So how did she seem to know so much?

Once she found the entryway, they crouched down to pry open the corner of the fencing. He touched her shoulder.

"Nadia stop."

He expected shock and possibly fear when he called her by name, instead she turned toward him with a twinkle in her eyes.

"You already know my name."

He nodded. "I do. How did you know mine?"

"We can talk later. Come with me."

He followed her through the fence and into the compound. As they neared the building, he noticed a warm glow at the bottom seam of the door. His ears twitched beneath his cap. Were there others?

Nadia rapped her knuckles to the tune of Silent Night on the door and waited. Footsteps echoed on the other side, followed by the scraping sound of furniture being moved. When it finally opened, he found himself staring at five disheveled teenagers.

"What's going on here, Nadia?" He asked.

"We help each other."

Noel looked from one dirty face to another, his heart constricting in his chest. There were so many in need. Every year more hope trickled away. The elves couldn't possibly save all the lost souls, not even with the magic of Christmas flowing in their veins. It was hopeless.

He was hopeless.

A boy stepped forward. "Are you an elf?"

Noel nodded. "I am."

The youth grinned at the others before meeting his eyes again. "We have something to show you."

Noel frowned. These young people obviously needed his help. But none of them seemed to realize it.

The boy held a candle and led him through the abandoned hallways. Noel sneezed when the stench of mold and dust hit his nostrils. Water dripped somewhere deeper within their makeshift fortress.

This was no place for young people to spend Christmas.

They turned a final corner into a long forgotten conference room. Seated around the table were four more adolescents. A few tiny candles flickered and the warm light danced over their work.

Toys.

Noel blinked back tears and shook his head. These weren't new toys. They were forgotten cast offs, but each child was hunched over their station, meticulously tightening screws, and using a plastic strip of paint-by-number tubs to touch up chipped paint.

"Nadia told us you'd come."

"You're making toys," Noel whispered.

One of them nodded. "Nadia has been collecting cans and recycling them. We use the money to get supplies from the thrift store to fix them up."

Noel shook his head. "I don't understand."

His guide chuckled. "It might not look like the factory at the North Pole, but it beats sitting around foster homes all night."

Noel looked up into the eyes of a very wise fourteen year old boy. He touched his hand and saw his mother leaving a baby for her own mother to raise. His grandmother passed away last year. Michael was alone in the world now.

"So you all meet here to make toys."

Tentative nods followed around the table. Nadia walked up behind him.

"I had a dream you were coming. We didn't think you'd be able to find us."

Noel spun around, speechless for a moment. He shook his head. "I don't understand.

Why are you doing this?"

She shrugged. "We're planning on dropping off a bag of toys at the juvenile center. Most of us have spent a Christmas or two there."

Her eyes went vacant again and Michael continued. "We figured we'd help Santa out this year. We know they're not the best toys, but at least the kids will have something, you know?"

A sparkle of magic rolled down Noel's cheek. "These are, most definitely, the best toys." He made eye contact with every child seated around the dusty table. "Gifts given out of love, not duty, are the most precious of all. Gifts given without expectation of anything in return."

His tear hit the floor, splashing a drop of magic under their feet. The bruised and broken toys glowed, sparks flickered around the table, and the dust disappeared, leaving behind new tools, paints and paintbrushes.

The young ones grinned at one another.

"You can't tell anyone about what you've seen." Noel kept his voice even and commanding. "Faith is what gives Christmas magic its power. If you look for answers you may break the spell."

"Who would believe us?" A young lady with a baseball cap grinned from the far end of the table.

Noel tipped his head to the wise youth. "Merry Christmas."

"Merry Christmas," they replied in unison.

He made his way through the darkened hallway to find Nadia leaning against the wall staring out into the night.

"Thank you," she whispered.

"For what?"

"For the magic."

He took her hand. "You and your friends are the real magic, Nadia."

She blinked and stared down at him. "We're just kids."

"No." He shook his head. "You're so much more. You and your fiends are *hope* for a brighter future. There is no greater gift."

Noel quietly left the teens to their work, exiting back into the darkness with hope burning deep in his heart.

He understood now.

He hadn't been sent on this business trip to save these children.

He was sent so the children could save him.

The End

The Demon's Christmas

Sheelak loved Christmas. He couldn't help it. Christmas was a guilty pleasure. Maybe it was the shiny decorations, or the secret gifts, or the delicious candy. He even loved the Christmas carols, although he had to sing quietly.

Demons had incredible hearing. One "Joy to the World" and his five-hundred-year-old-demon-butt would be banished back to Hell in a millisecond.

He shuddered at the thought. He liked being in the human world. They didn't have sweets and energy drinks back in the underworld. They had flames and hot steaming pools of boiling water reeking of sulphur.

And no Christmas. No gifts, no stockings, no trees, and definitely no singing.

"No fun," he muttered, climbing down his step ladder. Sheelak took a step back to admire his tree.

His black scarred wings fluttered behind him. He tilted his head, narrowing his protruding eyes. The star at the top still leaned toward the right, but he could live with that.

Close enough, he thought.

Now for the gifts. Ok gift. It was a tough year for a four foot tall demon in a human world.

He carefully lifted the box from the plastic Rite-Aid bag and grinned. Just what he wanted. In a flurry of cutting, creasing, and taping, the box was wrapped. He plucked out a bow and pressed it into place.

"Gift for Sheelak," he announced, tucking it under the tree.

Rubbing his gnarled hands together, his lips parted in a pointy-toothed grin. He couldn't wait to open it! But it was still Christmas Eve he needed to be patient. Waiting was part of the fun.

He tottered over to his small stove to start the water for some hot cocoa when a loud bang echoed through his tiny apartment. Sheelak jumped, turning to face the door.

"Sheelak!" A deep voice bellowed. "Open this door before I rip it off the hinges."

His bulging eyes flicked from the door to his beautiful Christmas tree and back to the door again, and his tiny leathery heart pounded. What to do? Stall. Yes, definitely stall.

"Just a minute," he called out as he wobbled over to his petite Christmas tree. Grabbing the tree skirt, he gave it a yank and then tossed it up over the branches, fighting to hide his homemade ornaments.

"You don't have a minute, Pond Scum. I'm coming in."

Sheelak gasped. His apartment door popped free of its hinges and a hulking black demon walked through the threshold.

"Durlu. H-hello. What brings you here?"

He watched Durlu's tongue flicking past his thin lips while he stalked around Sheelak's tiny studio apartment. Good thing he hadn't gotten the cocoa mixed yet or Durlu would have smelled it for sure. A tiny sigh of relief escaped him as he glanced over at his tree. Uh oh. Would the tree smell?

Sheelak unfolded his wings behind him, fluttering as he clasped his hands over the top of his round belly. "'Scuse me, Durlu. But why are you here? Is s-s-something wrong?"

"That's what I'm checking out, Worm."

Sheelak flinched at the name calling. He was a demon, sure. But a worm? He sighed.

Durlu was a bully. Nothing worse than a demon bully. Not only were they mean, but they could back it up too. Best not to stand up to them. Best to stay out of their way.

"I haven't done anything," Sheelak stammered. "I'm doing my job."

Durlu glared at him with beady red eyes. "Your job, Toilet Bowl, is to lose school children's homework. Stupid job for a demon if you ask me, but either way I haven't heard any crying kids lately so I'm here to check it out."

"Oh I see." Sheelak tried to mask his sudden wave of relief. "All the kids are on winter break from school, so there isn't any homework for me to take. They're not crying because they're waiting for Santa."

He almost reached up to cover his own mouth. Did he just say "Santa" out loud? Judging by the narrowing of Durlu's eyes he had. Sheelak cringed when the bully stepped even closer.

"What did you say?"

"Nothing."

"You said..."

"No I didn't."

"Yes, you did. You aren't celebrating in here, are you?"

"Celebrating what?" Sheelak replied, keeping his bulgy eyes downcast.

Durlu caught him by the neck and lifted

him up off the floor. Sheelak's tongue popped out past his pointed teeth as he gasped for air.

"Are you celebrating Christmas again, Sheelak?"

He shook his head so vigorously that his brain felt bruised. "No," he gasped. "Not me. It's forbidden."

Durlu nodded and released his hold. Sheelak crashed to the floor in a tangled heap.

"It is forbidden," Durlu said. "And yet..." He walked into the cozy kitchen and lifted the kettle as he glared at Sheelak. "...you're in here alone... Cooking?"

"Just a little cocoa. It's cold outside."

Durlu's black brow jutted up. "Cocoa?"

"Yes, humans like it. I thought I'd give it a try."

He slammed the kettle back on the stove and stalked back over to Sheelak. "What is wrong with you, Mosquito Larvae? You have a simple job to do here. Don't mess everything up by celebrating human holidays. My tail is on the line here too, do you understand? You know what Christmas celebrates, right? A savior for humankind. It's not like Halloween."

Sheelak nodded. "I know."

"Do you?" Durlu stared at the draped tree.

Sheelak rushed over to put his squatty body between Durlu and the tree. He puffed out his chest and raised his arms to keep the larger demon away from his hidden treasure.

"I understand," Sheelak said. "Now you should go so I can fix my door."

"Is that what I think it is?"

"What?"

Durlu rolled his red eyes. "Behind you."

"Behind me?" A bead of sweat trailed down Sheelak's brow.

"Yes behind you, Dung Beetle. Is that what I think it is?"

He shrugged and used the last of his magic reserves. "If you think it's my pet sewer rats then I guess you're right."

"Sewer rats?" Durlu reached over Sheelak's head and lifted the drape.

Sheelak squeezed his eyes shut, hoping for the best.

Grunting, Durlu released the drape and stepped back. "This isn't over, Duck Snot. Not til the fat lady sings!"

"What?"

"It means... Never mind," Durlu said, heading for the door. "I'll be watching you, Nose Wart."

And then he was gone. Sheelak puffed out a sigh of relief and peeked under the tree skirt. His Christmas tree twinkled back at him. His magic worked!

"Christmas miracle," he grumbled as he lifted up his door and propped it up against the jamb.

With the door temporarily fixed, he plucked the tree skirt off of his little tree and wrapped it back around the bottom like he'd seen them do on the Charlie Brown Christmas Special. He stood back to admire it again. Durlu just didn't understand. He'd probably never received a gift before. If he had felt the colorful paper ripping under his calloused fingers, and seen the way the ornaments on the tree sparkled, or tasted the delicious sweet hot cocoa, maybe then he'd see why Sheelak celebrated.

Halloween was fun. He could go out without his human disguise. In fact, people complimented him on his "costume". But he played pranks all year long, and he always looked like a demon, so Halloween almost felt like a normal day.

Christmas was different.

Christmas was full of special one-time-of-year things, like Santa and Christmas carols and gifts and candies. Being forbidden made it even more delicious. After all, he *was* a demon.

He grinned and went to the stove to warm up his cocoa. While the water heated, he grabbed his water can and carefully watered his Chia shelf. Another guilty pleasure. He had the Chia pig, turtle, frog, hippo, professor, and over there, wrapped and placed under the tree was his brand new Chia Shrek.

He couldn't wait to open it! An ogre Chia was probably the closest to a demon that he would ever find.

When the kettle started to whistle, a tiny sound caught his attention. Sheelak snatched the kettle from the stove and waited. A soft knock echoed through the room. His brow furrowed. It couldn't be Durlu, he already broke the door down once. He wouldn't have bothered to knock.

"Who's there?" he called.

"Mr. Sheelak? It's me, Cindee."

He grabbed his trench coat and quickly slid his arms inside, covering his wings. Next he put on his hat to cover his little horns. His disguise was far from perfect. Usually he'd wear gloves and a scarf too, but he didn't have time. He'd get rid of her quickly anyway.

Sheelak carefully lifted the door to the side and stared down at the little girl on his doorstep. She gave him a toothless grin, proudly showing him the tooth fairy's handiwork, and offered up a plate of gingerbread men.

"Merry Christmas, Mr. Sheelak. My Mom made the cookies for all the tenants. I decorated them myself."

Sheelak reached out with trembling fingers

to take the plate of homemade treats. "For me?"

"Yep."

He stared at the tiny men with crooked frosting smiles and missing red hot buttons and grinned at the girl. "Thank you."

"You're welcome." She frowned a little. "What happened to your door?"

"Oh it's nothing," he said. "It just came loose I guess."

"It's not loose, Mr. Sheelak. It's off. Want me to have my Mom call the repair guy? He can fix it for you."

"I'll fix it," he answered without taking his eyes off the Christmas cookies. "Do you want some cocoa?"

"Ummmm." Her foot started to scrape against the floor. "I'm not 'aposed to go in people's apartments."

He nodded, "Yes I guess that's a good rule. You never know what kind of demons you might run across, but I'd like to give you something."

And then he realized what he'd said was true. He *did* want to give her something. Odd.

Her little face brightened. "You got somethin' for me?"

"Yes!"

Wait. He didn't have anything for her. Did he? Sheelak stepped back from the door, allowing her to race inside.

"Oh you got a pretty tree, Mr. Sheelak!"

He nodded. "Thank you I..." His gaze fell on the brightly wrapped gift. His Chia. No, he couldn't. He wanted that. But he was already reaching for it. No! What was he doing? "This is for you Cindee."

Oh no! He gave his beautiful present away. No! He wanted to yank it back, but the joy on her face stopped him faster than a ball of fire from the devil himself.

Her big blue eyes stared up at him as she spoke. "For me? Really?"

He nodded and watched as she made quick work of the wrapping paper, squealing with delight.

"It's a Shrek! One of those things like on tv! I'll get to cut his hair, right?"

"Yes," he said. "It's a Chia pet."

"Ch-ch-ch-chia!" she sang.

"Exactly!" Sheelak laughed.

"Thank you, Mister Sheelak." She gave him a quick hug. "Can't wait to show my Mom! Merry Christmas!"

She ran off before he could return her greeting. Sheelak stared at his tree in stunned silence, unable to wipe the goofy smile off his round face. What was wrong with him? He'd just given away the gift he had wanted all year. And he felt...

Good?

Amazing in fact. Better than when he stole entire science projects.

A crooked smile tweaked the corner of his mouth. If one gift felt this good, how incredible would it be to give twenty?

Hmm...

He slid on his gloves and reached for his scarf. There wasn't any homework to steal right now anyway, right?

Stealing toys from stores on Christmas Eve would be equally as wicked. Durlu wouldn't have to know he was going to turn around and give them to children.

The kids would think the gifts were from Santa, and Durlu would think he was finally acting like a demon.

Perfect.

No one would ever have to know how good it felt to give a gift. It would be his little secret.

Another guilty pleasure.

He couldn't wait...

The End

Acknowledgements

This project was a labor of love and would have been impossible without the support of many people.

Thank you to all my Blogophilia family! You took me in on MySpace and cheered me on during my 52 stories in 52 weeks challenge. Your inspiration, comments and camaraderie made my writing journey such a joy! You're the best!

Thanks to my daughter, Panda, for allowing me to use her photo of the forgotten carnation for the cover.

She took the picture for her photography class, and it really spoke to me about forgotten beauty.

I couldn't have gotten this book printed without the help of my amazing Mom, Ally Benbrook. She helped me with the layout, saving me from throwing my computer across the room when I couldn't get Word 2010 to cooperate.

I'm also grateful to Tishia from ParaGraphic Design. She took my book cover concept and the mood for the anthology and ran with it, and I love the end result.

My husband also deserves a shout out for this anthology. He was my first-reader for many of these stories, and his opinions, encouragement and feedback mean the world to me.

Lastly, when I started to put this anthology together, I realized it was too large a project to handle on my own. Jennifer Morris from Books-a-Million stepped up and edited *every* story for me.

Thanks to her meticulous efforts, sentences were streamlined and the stories shine. I couldn't have pulled this together without her help.

Thank you so much for reading!

Poof

Made in the USA
Charleston, SC
17 January 2012